"You still work at the ranch?"

"When my dad needs me. But that is not what we are going to talk about right now."

The heat came on as Andres started the engine. Cat's hands had become cold without her noticing. Cat opened her mouth, but not a single word came out. There were so many words. Too many. Which ones would make this easier?

She loved his family so much. They had given her a safe harbor without asking questions. Family was so important to them that they would see her decision not as protecting everyone, but as a betrayal.

Bowing her head, she prayed. Her focus needed to be on God. He would give her the words. "You have a daughter."

She opened her eyes but kept her head down. Waiting for the explosion.

Nothing.

Cautiously, she raised her gaze and found him staring at her. Just staring.

"We have a daughter. My daughter, Willa, isn't Brad's. She's yours."

A seventh-generation Texan, **Jolene Navarro** fills her life with family, faith and life's beautiful messiness. She knows that as much as the world changes, people stay the same: vow-keepers and heartbreakers. Jolene married a vow-keeper who shows her holding hands never gets old. When not writing, Jolene teaches art to teens and hangs out with her own four almost-grown kids. Find Jolene on Facebook or her blog, jolenenavarrowriter.com.

Books by Jolene Navarro

Love Inspired

Cowboys of Diamondback Ranch

The Texan's Secret Daughter
The Texan's Surprise Return
The Texan's Promise
The Texan's Unexpected Holiday
The Texan's Truth
Her Holiday Secret

Lone Star Legacy

Texas Daddy
The Texan's Twins
Lone Star Christmas

Lone Star Holiday
Lone Star Hero

Visit the Author Profile page
at Harlequin.com for more titles.

Her Holiday Secret

Jolene Navarro

LOVE INSPIRED
INSPIRATIONAL ROMANCE

LOVE INSPIRED®
INSPIRATIONAL ROMANCE

ISBN-13: 978-1-335-40950-8

Her Holiday Secret

Copyright © 2021 by Jolene Navarro

This edition published by arrangement with Harlequin Books S.A.

For questions and comments about the quality of this book, please contact us
at CustomerService@Harlequin.com.

Love Inspired
22 Adelaide St. West, 40th Floor
Toronto, Ontario M5H 4E3, Canada
www.Harlequin.com

Printed in U.S.A.

Be of good courage, and he shall strengthen
your heart, all ye that hope in the Lord.
—*Psalm* 31:24

This is dedicated to the amazing women
I gained as sisters when I married Fred
Navarro: Gela, Vickie, Juanita, Pam, Linda, Leti,
Ann, Debra and Letty. Leti, Debra and Letty,
I'll see you on the dance floor soon.
Hope the others can join us.

Chapter One

Andres Sanchez followed Sam, the grounds manager, out of the stadium. They were always the last to leave. His long-sleeved shirt didn't do much to keep the chill out. This was his favorite season, and he loved being the announcer at the local football games.

But the excitement of the drummers, cheerleaders, fans and players had faded, leaving the sounds of nature to dominate.

He tilted his head up. The bright lights of Friday night were shut off, allowing the stars to take him to the edge of the universe. One deep breath and the salt air of the Texas coast filled his senses.

After thriving on the noise of the crowd, now he soaked in God's perfection. He should forget this nagging restlessness that tapped at him. But it wasn't working tonight.

"The sky is something, isn't it? That boy of mine said you were going to join him tomorrow at the airport. Parker loves his helicopters. He still pestering you to join that firefighting crew of his?"

With a chuckle, Andres nodded. "Yes, to all the above." At one time, he had had dreams of escaping and flying around the world, but those dreams had morphed into a simpler life. He had grown up and he wouldn't be leaving. His family needed him. The town needed him. When he had been at his lowest, they had stepped up and supported him.

Being a sheriff's deputy in his small community by the sea made him happy. This restlessness would pass. The only thing missing was a family of his own.

He wanted a connection with someone like his parents had.

It was only worse today because she was back. Catalina Wimberly. He glanced at his phone. She had called again. Why was she back after six years of silence?

She had been his best friend for so long. Then he'd made the mistake of expecting more. Two weeks of perfection, then he had lost her without knowing why. Was she home for the holidays? Was it her father's health? His thumb hovered.

A tiny part of his stupid heart wanted answers.

Nope. He was not going to reply. If it had to do with her family's ranch, his father was the Wimberly foreman. They should call him.

His mom had also left a message. Another daughter or cousin of a friend she wanted him to meet. Maybe he should call Vanessa again. They had gone on a couple of nice dates. She wasn't too bad.

With a grunt, he shook his head. He wanted more than *not bad.*

He didn't have the energy to deal with any of this tonight.

Six years ago, Cat had walked away from him, and he was over her. He was. Or maybe he was lying to himself and he had never taken his heart back.

His gut twisted. Why was Cat in town?

Thoughts of her didn't fill his brain anymore. Not every day, anyway. The unanswered questions had stopped taunting him in the late hours of the night.

He had given everything to his family as his mother went through all the treatments to knock the cancer out of her body. Thankfully, his mom had won that battle, but he had lost the remains of his heart when Cat abandoned him.

He had needed her, and she had fled back to school in California, disappearing from his life. More than disappeared.

The town gossips couldn't tell him fast

enough that she had gotten engaged to another man.

She couldn't take a minute to explain what he had done wrong. Other than being the son of her father's ranch hand.

What he struggled with the most was why she had given herself to him completely, only to run away the next morning. Had she just felt sorry for him?

The pity in everyone's eyes, when the engagment was announced, was doubled when they heard that the couple was expecting a baby. Hiding wasn't an option and to make it worse they brought him casseroles as if someone had died.

His gut twisted.

Cat had been his friend for years, and it had felt so natural to fall in love with her. He should have known better. They were from different worlds. He bit down with his back molars, grinding his teeth. *Stop thinking about her. It doesn't matter.*

"Sanchez?" Sam said his name as though

he had been trying to get his attention for a while now.

"Yeah. Just thinking."

"Careful. That's a dangerous activity for a man, especially if it has to do with a woman. I hear the Wimberly girl is back."

With his eyes closed, Andres groaned to the sky. The locals knew him too well. He definitely had a love-hate relationship with his hometown. "I'm fine."

"Okay then, you have a good night." With a wave, Sam went left toward the old field house. Andres watched until he disappeared into the darkness. A few minutes later, headlights came on and the older man drove off.

With Sam safely on his way home, Andres turned right, then paused. His truck should be the only vehicle in the parking lot. The term "parking lot" was used loosely. It was more of a large pasture with beaten-down grass.

There was an older Civic he didn't recognize parked on the other side of his Ford.

A woman pulled on his door handle. He froze. His lungs stopped working. Catalina.

Even with her back to him, there was no doubt it was her. He hated that he knew her so well. Worse, there was a small, traitorous part of his heart that slammed with excitement and maybe a tinge of joy. The stupid organ must have amnesia to forget the pain she'd caused.

Andres was tired and didn't want to deal with her drama.

Not that it was her fault. She was who she was, and he was the one who had gotten caught up in a fantasy that would never be true. There was no way in this world Catalina Wimberly could ever be his. He had known that, but he had gotten all mixed up with the collision of grief and love.

"Are you trying to get arrested for car theft again?" he asked her as he neared.

She spun around with a squeal, planting a hand over her heart. Eyes closed, she took a few deep breaths. "You scared me." Big green eyes flashed open, hurt. The old wounds were still there. But the makeup was gone. He had always hated the heavy black liner she used to hide behind.

Gritting his teeth, he pushed back the instinctive response to reach out and soothe her. She was not his to heal.

Hands on her hips, Cat narrowed those bright green eyes at him. "That was a misunderstanding. Clair Dobson had told me Mr. Miller wanted his car moved. I was just…" She waved her hand as if she could shoo away any unpleasantness. "I'm not here to talk about the past. Well, I am, but not that past." She lowered her head, and when she brought her gaze up to meet his, he saw sadness and regret.

The full moon reflected off the light green of her eyes, the specks of gold flickering.

Nope. He needed to stay focused. He looked away. "Why are you breaking into my truck?"

"I wasn't breaking into anything. I didn't want to miss you. It was getting cold and I was going to wait for you. I can't believe you still have Ol' Blue."

"She works fine, and I don't throw things out just because I want something new. What do you want? I'm tired."

Looking at his truck over her shoulder, she chewed on her bottom lip. "Well, funny story." She laced her fingers together and stared at the stadium.

"What are you doing, Catalina? You went silent on me six years ago. Why now?"

She rubbed the back of her neck and shifted her gaze to the side.

He waited in the silence. Unfortunately, it gave him time and free space in his mind to study her features. She looked... beautiful and fresh. And unsure.

The full moon was so bright tonight he could see the natural highlights in the red curls that hung past her shoulders like fire. If he reached out, he could touch them. And get burned.

Last time he had seen her she had cut it off because her parents had wanted her to wear it long. She had told him that since she wasn't dancing anymore, she didn't need to keep it past her shoulders. Dancing had been another thing she had loved, then walked away from. That was what she did.

He had dreamed of being the one that would give her a reason to stay.

What was he doing? "It's late. There's a special alumni fifth quarter at the church tonight that I planned to stop by before going home."

"Do you still live with your parents at the ranch?"

"No." He shifted and looked at her. This was the moment he should get in his truck and leave. Unlike her, he always had a problem walking away. "I have a house on the edge of town." He pulled his keys from his pocket.

"That's nice." She moved a step forward, blocking his path. "We need to talk."

"If you want to apologize, I accept. We don't need to speak of it ever again. But I really need to go."

She reached out to touch his arm. The light contact stopped him. He kept his gaze on her hand. Looking up would be dangerous. "Cat, I'm not in the mood. There is nothing so important that it can't wait." And he lifted his face. For a moment, the world faded. In some ways she hadn't changed at all, but there were also subtle signs of the woman she'd become.

The little girl who followed him everywhere was long gone. Along with the lost teen who had needed a friend. She had a sister and brother, but they were more than a decade older and had moved out of the house before she turned eight.

He shook his head. His family had been there for her, and then she had left without a word during their darkest days. His heart had been crushed, but it wasn't the only one. She had hurt his family.

"Catalina. Go by and visit my mom." He

sighed. "She's missed you. She never understood why you left like you did." None of them had. "I have tomorrow off, so call me with a good time and place to meet and I'll be there." He'd cancel his fly time with Parker. Yep. He was weak.

"Every morning I woke up thinking of her, and every night she was in my prayers. I was so relieved when I heard she had beat the cancer."

"You should tell her that."

He moved around her to reach for his door. Looking over his shoulder was a mistake. Silhouetted by the round moon behind her, she looked so alone. She'd always been that way. Not fitting in with her family at the big house, and not quite a part of his family in the old ranch quarters.

"Your hair looks nice." It really did. The red strands fell in natural waves around her face and past her shoulders.

Her mother had complained about the red and had wanted her to tone it down to a nice blond. What had Cat done back then? She colored her hair, all right. With the rainbow. When her mother complained about the green, she made it purple. He had kind of liked the turquoise.

A smile pulled on his mouth at the memory. He forced himself to turn away and open his door before he did something really stupid. He should just go home, take a hot shower and clear his head. He had a feeling he wouldn't be getting any sleep tonight.

"Andres." Her hand touched the top of his. "Please. I promised God I would talk to you tonight."

He groaned. "Seriously? You're talking to God now? When did that start? Never mind." He rubbed his forehead. "I'm tired and not sure I can deal with whatever it is you think you have to tell me. Can it wait until tomorrow morning around nine? The Espinoza sisters have a bakery on the boardwalk. We could meet there."

"No." Looking frustrated, she pressed

her lips together and closed her eyes for a moment. "I meant, yes. We can meet there and talk, but I'm not leaving until I say what I have to tell you."

Pulling his hand away from hers, he got behind the steering wheel and slammed his keys into the ignition. He reached for his door to shut her out. He needed to leave for his sanity and the safety of his heart.

Her hand reached out and stopped him again. "You're a father. My daughter, Willa—she's your daughter."

The world around him blurred. He couldn't have heard right. No way. "Get in." His command was sharp and coated in a mix of anger and confusion. He didn't care. She had just told him that her daughter was his. Her five-year-old daughter. The child wasn't Brad's. She. Was. His.

She closed her eyes. The feel of his truck cab was so familiar it hurt. It still had a faint aroma of leather and hay. "You still work at the ranch?"

"When my dad needs me. But that is not what we are going to talk about right now."

The heat came on as he started the engine. Her hands had become cold without her noticing. She opened her mouth, but not a single word came out. There were so many words. Too many. Which ones would make this easier?

She loved his family so much. They had given her a safe harbor without asking questions. Family was so important to them that they would see her decision not as protecting everyone, but as a betrayal.

Bowing her head, she prayed. Her focus needed to be on God. He would give her the words. "You have a daughter."

She opened her eyes but kept her head down. Waiting for the explosion.

Nothing.

Cautiously, she raised her gaze and

found him staring at her. Just staring. His mouth opened, then closed.

"We have a daughter. My daughter, Willa, isn't Brad's. She's yours."

Both hands on the steering wheel, he turned his gaze from her to the darkness in front of them.

"I don't understand." His knuckles were white. "How do you know she's not Brad's?"

"Brad and I were never together in any way."

He laughed. It was a hollow sound. "You were engaged. Other than marriage, that's about as together as two people can get."

"That night, after we found out your mom had cervical cancer. Do you remember?"

Jaw hard, he glared at her. "You mean the worst night of my life, when I found out my mother might die of cancer and then you disappeared? Yeah. I remember that night. You wouldn't answer my calls. Didn't return a single text. When I went to your house, your father made it very clear you were about to get a restraining order if I didn't stop harassing you. He threatened my parents and my future with the air force."

"A future that you didn't—" She closed her eyes and focused on the reason she was here. She had done this for him, and he hadn't even gone to the academy. "That night. My father saw you leaving my room. He was so angry. Angrier than I had ever seen him, and I'd seen him angry so many times. It was made very clear that I was to never see you again. You had a future in the air force to make something of your life." The pressure on her chest squeezed. *One. Two. Three.*

"He said I had to grow up and stop being impulsive and selfish. There were plans in place and I was…" Her heart twisted at the words her father had said to her that night. Each word cold and hateful, but she couldn't go there.

"Since when did you do anything your father wanted you to do?"

"Since he threatened you and your family. He told me his connections got you into the Air Force Prep School and he could get you kicked out. If he fired your father, your parents would lose their income and their home here on the ranch. At the time, all I could think about was the insurance they would need with your mother's diagnosis." Tears burned her throat and eyes. She couldn't cry.

Digging her nails into her palms, she stared at the stadium. Empty and dark. "He sent me back to school in California the next day. Then a few weeks later he made sure I went to the doctor." She wrapped her arms around her middle. "When the test came back positive, he gave me two choices. To end the pregnancy or marry his guy Brad. I was so scared for you and me. For your whole family. I didn't have a choice. I couldn't hurt our baby."

"Cat." He put his hand on her shoulder. "You had another choice. I would have helped."

"At the expense of your mother's life? And did you know that if you have a dependent, you can't go to the Air Force Academy? I looked it up to make sure he wasn't lying to me. You had worked so hard at school to get ahead. You were top of your class." Shaking her head, she huddled against the door, putting as much space between them as she could. "I didn't want to be the reason your dreams were ruined. I had to protect you and our baby."

"Willa?" The single word was said in awe.

At the thought of her daughter—their daughter—her chest lightened. "Yes. Here." Digging through her purse, she looked for her phone. "They were both horrible choices. Once I calmed down, stopped crying and thought it through, I realized my father couldn't force me do either of those things. Poor Brad was re-lieved that I refused to marry him."

"Poor Brad?" His fist clenched the steer-ing wheel. "The man was marrying a woman who was pregnant with someone else's baby to gain favor from your father. Why? So he could get a bigger office and a fancy title?"

She didn't want to fight over Brad. He'd been very decent to her, and he looked like the jerk who abandoned his child when they called off the impromptu en-gagement. Of course, he still got the big-ger office and *V.P.* added to his door.

"Here." Wanting to move the conversa-tion away from Brad, she thrust the most recent picture of Willa at Andres. "That was taken a couple of days ago at the park outside our condo in Austin."

"Willa?" His face softened as he stud-ied the picture.

"I named her after you. I didn't want it to be too obvious, so I took your middle name, Guillermo, and gave her the female version. Willemina." Pressure on her chest made breathing hard as she watched him touch the screen. Moisture pooled in his eyes.

"Willa." His gaze darted to her. "Wait, you named her Willemina Wimberly?"

She grimaced. "When I picked the name, I was thinking of Sanchez. Of course, legally I couldn't just throw your name on the birth certificate. Her full name is Willemina Francisca Wimberly."

"You named her after my mother, too?"

"Yes. I hope that's okay. I wanted her to have a connection to your family, but I didn't know how. That was all I had at the time."

"Your mother knows she's mine?"

"No. I didn't want anyone to know until I told you. She never asks questions. My father was furious at the name. For a month, he avoided her, but she's their first grandchild, and Mom was confused by his reaction. Surprisingly, she's been our biggest supporter. I wouldn't have been able to stay in school without her help. I was able to do an internship with an international company that designs mobile games and apps. I work for them now. I get to work from home and make my own hours." She bit her lip. Tonight was not the time to tell him that she might be moving to Canada.

"Home? In Austin?" He had a dazed look in his eyes she had only seen one other time. The horrible night his mother had told him about the cancer.

She nodded. "Yes. My mom really has been a great help in so many ways. She spends the week with me, then goes to Houston for the weekends. She's very close to Willa. But now she's blaming herself for my dad's health problems."

"We would have helped you. My mom could be close to her, too." Resentment brewed in the depth of those dark eyes.

"I told you, I couldn't risk your family. There was so much at stake."

"*Familia* is everything. She's also my

parents' first grandchild. They would have done anything for her. We would have made it work no matter what your father did to us."

"I know. But at the time, I was so afraid of him. I was only eighteen, and he was bigger than life. I've grown up so much since then."

"I want to see her." He handed back her phone. "My parents will want to meet her."

"Of course. That's why I'm here."

With a curt nod, he gripped the steering wheel. "When?"

"Tomorrow. You can bring them to the house."

"No. My parents' house. They won't feel comfortable in the big house."

"I never felt at ease there either." She tried to smile but gave up. "We'll come down around ten?"

"How about you bring her for breakfast? My mom will want to feed her anyway."

"My best memories are breakfast in your mother's kitchen. All the noise and laughter. It was so different from my family meals."

They sat in silence as the wind picked up and pushed on his truck. He turned to her. "Is she okay? Has she been lonely or…?" He dropped his head for a moment. "You felt so unloved in all of your parents' homes."

"No. I have a small townhouse in Austin. No formal dining room. Not a single room she is not allowed to enter. There is nothing in my home that is more important than her. Believe it or not, my mom has been super supportive, and Willa has my dad wrapped around her little finger."

He swallowed and nodded. "You had such a cold childhood. It bordered on negligence."

"She's known nothing but love. I promise." She reached out and touched his arm. "I'm so sorry about how this has been handled. I'm here to make it right. When she was a baby, I found a good church home and they have been so kind to us. I'm in a much better place with God now. I know words are easy, but hopefully my actions will restore some of your trust. I'm sorry it took me so long to tell you. You were my best friend and I hope—" She clamped her teeth together and stopped talking.

He didn't care about her loneliness and isolation. Pulling the handle, she opened the door to get out. His hand on her shoulder held her in place.

"Thank you for bringing her home. I'll see you in the morning."

She pulled an envelope from her jacket, staring at it and trying to remember what she had written. Not quite making eye contact, she offered it to him. "This is a letter I wrote after I found out about her. I was so upset, and my father wouldn't allow me to talk to you, so I wrote you a letter. I was afraid if I mailed it, he would know. All my doubts and fears will be there. It might help you understand why I did what I thought was right at the time."

She looked him in the eye. "I know it

can't make up for the last five years of her life, but it's all I have to give. You can share it with your parents."

He took the letter. There was a tremor in his hands she had never seen before. "Thank you."

"Tomorrow."

"Seven." It sounded more like a command than a confirmation.

Giving him her best Ladies of Wimberly smile, she headed to her car.

His family was going to be shocked. She hoped they would see she was a new woman in Christ now and that she wanted to do the right thing.

Andres waited until she pulled into the street. Once she drove past him, she cried. The weight and stress emptied out of her. He knew the truth, and now her daughter would have the Sanchez family's love.

The one thing she had always wanted was now forever out of her reach. To be a part of their family. To be loved by Andres. Those were childhood dreams that could never come true. She would always be on the outside looking in.

They would all hate her now, and rightfully so.

They wouldn't hate Willa. She would get all their love. Her daughter would get to meet the family she always wanted but could never have. If she did receive that promotion, Willa and she would be moving to Canada. It was too good of an opportunity to pass on.

But if they were going to be that far away, her daughter needed time to know Andres and his family.

The holidays were the perfect opportunity to spend time together as a family. Willa was all that mattered now.

Chapter Two

Andres couldn't breathe. He didn't bother driving to his house in town. There was only one place he would be tonight. Giving her a bit of time to get down the street, he waited so that she wouldn't think he was following her.

Then he drove the same road, along the Gulf. The Wimberly ranch was almost twenty miles north of town. But he wasn't going to the big house.

Nope. Once past the huge stone-and-wrought-iron entrance, he made a left off the paved driveway. A mile down the rough dirt road, he arrived at the place where he grew up. His father had worked on the ranch for years before Andres was born. When he'd turned four, his father had been promoted and given this house to live in. It was his childhood home, but it would always belong to the Wimberly family.

There was no way he could sleep without telling his parents they had a granddaughter. A five-year-old granddaughter. A deep sadness settled heavily at all the things he'd missed. This was not how it was supposed to happen.

The envelope kept pulling his attention. Reading it might give him answers to many of his questions, but was he ready to know how scared and lonely she had been? He knew himself well enough to know he'd feel sorry for her. She had run away with his daughter. Forgiveness was not what he wanted to give her. Not yet.

The Wimberlys were the most entitled people he had ever met. Now they had kept the one thing from him that was most important. His daughter.

He had just turned eighteen when he had come home for the holidays from the Air Force Academy Preparatory School. His parents had been so proud when Mr. Wimberly helped him get into the school. It was going to be the first step in achieving his dream of being a fighter pilot.

His first day home, Cat had come prancing in like she always did whenever she was at the ranch. She hated the formality of her family's dining room. Cat had been standing in the sun-filled little kitchen helping his mother roll out tortillas. Seeing her short curls pulled off her face with a pink headband, a face free of makeup, he had been struck mute.

His mother laughed as Cat tried to sharpen her Spanish. How had he never noticed her like that before? By the end of the week, he had fallen in love with her. She had given him the best two weeks of his life. They had flirted, gone to a few movies and hung out. They had fit. She was everything he had wanted in a partner. He had fallen hard.

Then, right before he was due to go back to school in January, his parents had sat the family down and told them of their mother's diagnosis.

Cervical cancer. She would have surgery in a week, then start chemo treatments.

As the eldest of four, he knew the others relied on him to be calm. His parents counted on him to take care of his siblings. His mother was scared. His father looked so lost.

There was only one person he could fall apart in front of. Cat.

For the first time ever, he sneaked into the big house. He'd tapped on Cat's window, and she'd let him in. She had been just as devastated at the news. He had foolishly thought that with her by his side, they could conquer anything. Even his mother's cancer.

With one last kiss before the sun came up, he climbed out the window and walked to his parents' house. Hope had been restored.

He snorted. He'd been a complete idiot to trust her.

January. That was the last time he saw her. He'd been so angry at God for the cervical cancer his mother was going to have to fight, but he'd thought he had Catalina in his corner.

In their shared anguish, he had crossed the line that night and he had completely given himself to her and he thought she had done the same. But it had been one-sided. She had just pitied him.

He'd never understood why she had left the following day without a word to him. She was just gone.

When she wouldn't return his texts or answer his calls, he couldn't believe it. At one point, he almost dropped out of school. He was so desperate to be home with his family and to talk to Cat.

But then the announcement came that she would be marrying one of her dad's prodigies in Houston.

A Yale graduate with a business degree and a VP title in her father's company. Not that Andres had stalked him. Much.

It was easy information to find out. It wasn't like he'd hacked into any secret files or accounts. He was checking both of their social media updates every hour. When he'd realized what he was doing, Andres deleted all his social media accounts.

At that point, he doubted everything that had happened between them. It had to have been all in his head, one-sided.

Had she already been dating Brad in Houston? She was bored easily. Maybe he'd just been a diversion while she was on the ranch, like the horses or her dancing. She eventually would lose interest.

He gave all his energy to his family and school. It had taken some time, but he had realized a few things about himself.

The dreams of going out into the world had been others' plans for him. He wanted to be a family man and stay where he was needed.

Worse, he had fallen in love with her, forgetting who she really was. As much as Cat claimed to love the ranch and Port Del Mar, it would never be her permanent home. She was too grand for this shoebox of a town.

He belonged in this town. He thanked God in his daily prayers that his mother was in remission and that he had the opportunity to stay close to family and have a job protecting them and Port Del Mar before he had fully committed to the air force.

The only thing that had been missing was a family of his own. But now he had a daughter. Without a wife. Not the way he'd imagined starting a family. A daughter who lived in Austin with Catalina Wimberly.

As he pulled up to his parents' house, the front porch light came on. No matter how much had changed in the last six years, some things were constant. Like his family's love and support.

They would always be there for him. He wanted the kind of marriage his parents lived every day.

Catalina sat in the dark room watching her daughter sleep. Willa was surrounded by a herd of stuffed animals, lined up in a neat row so they could say their prayers together. The room was quiet.

She was the reason she was doing this. Willa needed to know her father before she got any older. And with the possibility of the job new taking her to Canada, time was running out. Her father's recent brush with death proved that tomorrow wasn't guaranteed.

She had done the right thing telling Andres. Now she had to tell her mom, and in the morning, she would have to look Franny Sanchez in the eye and ask for forgiveness.

Leaning over, she gave her daughter a gentle kiss on her forehead, then headed downstairs.

Telling Andres had been the hardest. She had wanted to fall in front of him and beg forgiveness. To tell him that each of his messages back then had made her cry.

On the worst nights, she would listen to his voice over and over as he pleaded with her to call him. He begged because he worried about her. He told her he was sorry for whatever he'd done. His voice had broken her heart. But she knew his words had come from a place of guilt and he would move on. Better without her. His mother would have the insurance she needed.

She still had the old phone even though the message were long gone.

She rubbed her burning eyes. The young girl she was had allowed her father to control and manipulate her into doing what he thought was best. He was the great Calvin Wimberly and could do no wrong.

But she wasn't a scared teenager anymore, and that larger-than-life man was fighting to keep his heart pumping.

She paused outside the door to his study, which was now equipped with all the medical supplies he needed to stay alive. He hadn't wanted to be trapped in the city or upstairs, so he had demanded that his study at the ranch be turned into his sickroom.

The only time she had been allowed in his sanctuary was when he had heard rumors of her tarnishing the family name. The Wimberly legacy was always to be upheld and protected. She hadn't been a very good soldier in her father's army.

She heard the soft humming of the oxygen machine that her father now needed 24/7. The huge oak desk had been pushed back, away from the large wall of windows. A hospital bed took up the space now. If he got tired of looking out over his ranch, Calvin could study the floor-to-ceiling shelves full of books, pictures of the important people he shook hands with and trophies that proved he had done his part to build on the Wimberly legacy.

In the corner was a small round table with two comfortable chairs. Her mom hovered over her father, adjusting blankets that looked fine. For a moment, Catalina was a scared eight-year-old who just wanted her daddy's eyes to light up with love instead of disapproval.

When she had been diagnosed with ADD and dyslexia, her father had told her it was all in her head. With hard eyes, he had said, "There is no excuse for being lazy and undisciplined."

She started to back out, but her mother looked up. "Catalina. Come in. I'm glad you're back. It took me a while to get Willa settled down. She was so excited about being here. Sleep was the last thing she wanted to do with the whole ranch to explore."

"She tried to convince me that we should sleep under the stars like the real cowboys. But she finally gave up the fight." She glanced at her father.

"He's sleeping." Her mother went to the table and sat in one of the chairs. "I was about to drink a cup of hot tea. Do you want some?"

"No, thank you." She took the chair opposite her mother. Laura Wimberly was the perfect model wife for a Texas oil baron and cattleman. Her golden-blond hair was smooth and framed her face in the most flattering way.

"Thank you so much for coming ahead and making sure the equipment had arrived. I know your father is pleased to finally have Willa on the ranch. I don't understand why you've kept her away so long. This used to be your favorite place on earth. How did your trip into town go? Everything all right?"

Had her mother really not figured it out? The unspoken rule was that nothing unpleasant was ever talked about. The uglier it was, the more it was ignored. "Mom, why have you never asked me about Willa's dad?"

"Your father told me she was Brad's, but that y'all had a falling-out."

"You had to know as soon as she was born that Brad couldn't be her father. He looks like a direct descendant of the first Vikings."

With a polite smile, her mother waved her hand around gracefully as if she could make the unpleasant words disappear. "We have Willa. That's all that is important. I learned a long time ago not to ask questions if I might not like the answers."

"So you knew Andres was her father?" Catalina sat back in her chair, not sure what to think.

Her mother's mouth dropped open. "Andres? Andres Sanchez? Jose's oldest boy?"

"Who did you think it was?"

The elegant hand waved without purpose again. "With your short attention span and impulsive behaviors, I was afraid to ask. You had been in California for a full semester." Her mother folded her hands and bowed her head as if praying.

After a few deep breaths, she lifted her eyes to meet Catalina's. "I'm sorry, sweetheart. I tend to think the worst with your past behaviors. But we have Willa now, and that is all that matters." She frowned. "Does Andres know? Does your father? I don't understand."

"Father knew from the beginning and orchestrated it so that no one else would know, including Andres. That was the reason I went into town. To tell Andres."

"Oh." Her mother took a sip of tea. It was a trick she used to collect and analyze appropriate responses. It was a skill she tried to teach Catalina, but she had never mastered it.

"That had to be a very difficult conversation. Your father needs to know. I'll call Daniel. We need legal advice."

"No. No lawyers. And I'm not talking to Father about this anymore."

Laura looked to the bed. "You might be

right about your father, but Daniel's our family lawyer."

"I don't care. It was wrong not to tell Andres. So I fixed that tonight. In the morning I'm going to take Willa to Franny and Jose's house."

Her mother reached over and gripped her hand. "Sweetheart, let's take our time and make sure it's done right. There is no way to know how they will react. We should have legal papers drawn up before you let Willa meet them."

"That just proves how little you know Andres and his family. If you knew them, you would know that *familia es todo*."

With an exasperated huff, her mother pulled away. "Yes, family is everything to us, too. But Willa has a routine. She has a set of grandparents she knows. This will just confuse her. It's two different worlds."

"*Family* as in the people. Not the legacy. They say it all the time and live by that. I'm not arguing about this. It's been too long already."

Her mother looked away, focusing on her father's breathing. If Catalina didn't know better, she would think those were tears in her mother's eyes, but Laura Crawford Wimberly never cried.

"Mother." She softened her tone. "I've been praying about this for a while. It's not a rash decision." She stood. "I promise it will be fine."

Catalina's stomach twisted. Hope that it would be fine was about as false as her mother's smile. "There's something else Franny Sanchez always said: '*Si Dios quiere.*'"

"What does that mean?"

"I think the literal translation is 'It's what God wants,' but she said it's more of a way to say, 'Trust God with everything. Even the bad works for the good.' I struggle with total faith sometimes."

"I trust God." Her mother sighed. "It's men I don't trust. We don't know how that Sanchez boy will react. Or his parents. This'll make our working relationship very awkward. This could hurt Willa."

"His name is Andres, and he is a grown man. I can't change the mistakes of the past, but I can make things right going forward. I've done the easy thing for too long. It's time to make this right. There is something else I need to tell you."

Her mother didn't say a word, but fear flashed in her eyes.

"I've been interviewed for a promotion at work. Instead of doing bits and pieces of projects, I would have creative control of new ideas and bringing them to life with a team."

Her mother relaxed. "Oh, dear, that sounds perfect for you."

"I think so. It's in Canada. I would have to move closer to the headquarters so that I actually go to the offices."

Her mother gasped. "Canada? Like the other country? You can't take Willa that far away."

"If I want to grow and be independent, this is a good move for me and Willa. But if I'm leaving Texas in the new year,

I have to give Andres and his family a chance to know Willa now. She's getting older and...well, it's the right thing to do."

"I'll go with you." Her mother lifted her chin.

"To Canada or the Sanchez house?"

"Both."

"No. Daddy needs you more than we do. And this is time for Willa to get to know the other half of her family. I don't want there to be any tension." Or as little as possible, anyway. "I have to do this on my own."

After kissing her silent mother on the cheek, she went to check on her father. His eyes fluttered open and he reached for her hand. "Love you, sweet girl." He took a breath, then licked his dry lips. She reached for the ChapStick and applied it. "Thank you," he rasped.

"Father, I told Andres. I'm taking Willa to meet her other grandparents in the morning."

Maybe she shouldn't have told him, but

she was so tired of hiding the truth. It was a dark and heavy way to live.

He sighed and nodded. "Good. It's past time."

That was not what she expected. With a kiss to his forehead, she left and headed up the grand staircase to her old room. She prayed that tomorrow would go well. She also prayed that God would show her the best time to tell Andres about Canada.

At this rate, he was going to hate her forever.

Chapter Three

"Mama. You're hurting my hand." Willa didn't pull her hand away, but she looked up at Catalina with questions in big dark eyes that looked so much like Andres's.

Relaxing her grip, Catalina smiled at her daughter. "Sorry, sunshine." She needed to calm down.

In a giant pink tutu and well-worn purple cowboy boots, her daughter was beyond adorable. Laura had, of course, questioned the choice, but Catalina loved the whimsical innocence of her daughter's outfit. She wished she had been able to wear it as a girl.

With a grin, she admitted silently that she'd like to wear it now. Occasionally those old ballerina dreams crept in. They hadn't been practical when she was younger, and they were even more of a waste of time now.

Maybe Willa should be in dance classes. Dance had brought her so much joy and emotional pain, but her daughter didn't have those scars.

She had hoped that walking to meet the Sanchez family would give her a chance to release the anxiety that had exploded since she'd come back to the ranch. Really, it had been hovering since she'd found out she was pregnant with Willa, never allowing her to truly be open and unhindered.

It might be corny, but she prayed that the truth would set her free. Her daughter deserved a fully present mother who loved her without fear. Willa deserved to be cherished by the Sanchez family, too.

There wasn't a doubt that they would

cherish her. They had been a bright spot in Catalina's lonely childhood. They had made her feel loved—and she hadn't even been theirs.

"Look!" Willa pulled her hand. "Flowers." Along the fence, a cluster of wildflowers grew.

"The yellow ones are small sunflowers, and the others are purple coneflowers."

"Can we pick some? I can give them to…" She blinked at her mother. "What do I call my other grandmother? Will she be GiGi, too?" She wrinkled her nose. "That'll get very confusing."

"She'll love the flowers. We can ask her what she wants to be called. I always imagined her as a Buelita."

"Buelita." She tested it out. "Is it like a short *abuelita*? That means *grandmother* in Spanish." She pulled the purple flowers first.

"It is." She had found a dual-language preschool and was amazed at what Willa had picked up. Most moms thought their children were smart, but in Willa's case it was true.

The thick sunflower stalks were too hard for Willa to break, so Catalina pulled out the pocketknife her brother had given her when she'd turned twelve. It was the only gift she had received from him, and she foolishly cherished it.

After gathering several of each kind of flower, Willa was ready to keep walking. "I like the yellow and purple together. Purple is my favorite color, but GiGi says it's tacky." She held the bouquet up for approval. "Is this too much purple?"

"GiGi has some ideas I don't agree with. You use whatever amount of purple you like."

"I think GiGi's feelings were hurt that you told her she couldn't come with us."

"I'll talk to her, but this is your opportunity to spend time with your other grandmother and grandfather."

"And my father. This is very exciting."

Willa had still been talking as she skipped ahead, the tutu flopping around her.

"It is." Knots pulled at her insides. Would the Sanchez family want custody? How would they work this out without putting stress on Willa? And if she moved to Canada? Maybe her mother was right and she needed to consult a lawyer.

Everything in her world was shifting. It was unavoidable, but she was still nervous what this meant for her and Willa.

They approached the small ranch house surrounded by a simple white picket fence. It had been built over a hundred years ago for the first Wimberlys who settled the land. The next generation had built the big house. Generations of history and legacy had been drilled into her. As though being a Wimberly made her better than other people.

Andres's truck was already here, even though she had come a little early, hoping to beat him. She should have known better.

They went through the freshly painted gate and entered a little brick courtyard surrounded by red, yellow and pink roses.

"Oh, it's so pretty. I hope she likes my flowers."

Together, they stepped onto the porch. "I'm sure she will love them." Raising her fist to knock on the faded blue door, she froze as it flew open.

"Hello!" Franny Sanchez, the matriarch of the Sanchez family, brimmed with excitement, her ever-present smile wider than normal. "Welcome. Welcome. Come in." Her warm golden-brown eyes stayed focused on Willa as she stepped back. Her black hair had streaks of gray. Being a couple of inches over five feet, she had always been small, but she seemed smaller now.

Willa held up her bundle of wildflowers after Franny closed the door. "These are for you. May I call you Buelita? Or would you rather I use another name? My name is Willemina Francisca Wimberly.

But everyone calls me Willa. I'm named after my daddy and you." Her daughter had never met a stranger. But in her protected world people were kind, so she had no reason to fear them.

"Oh my." Franny Sanchez went down on her knees and took the flowers. Her eyes clouded with tears, but her smile was huge and welcoming. Her stare was intense as she studied the details of her grandchild's features. She tucked a soft brown curl back from Willa's face. "You do look like your father."

She glanced up at Catalina, and some of the warmth went out of the kindest eyes Catalina had known growing up. Acid burned her stomach at the thought of disappointing this woman, who had been more of a mother to her than her own mother back then.

Focusing her attention back on Willa, Franny took the flowers. "These are the prettiest things I've ever seen other than you. I would love for you to call me Buel-ita, *mija*."

Willa giggled. "That means *my little girl* or *sweet daughter*, right?"

Andres's father approached and rested his working hands on the base of his wife's neck. His broad shoulders matched his son's. Thick dark hair with no evidence of graying was brushed back from a handsome face that showed the signs of a life lived outdoors. "It does. Call me Buelito. I love your boots."

"Thank you, Buelito. It's a great pleasure to meet you. Is my father here? I would very much like to see him."

"Listen to you sounding so grown and with such nice manners." Franny stood. "Let's put these in water."

"GiGi says good manners are a sign of proper breeding." Willa followed the couple into the kitchen area.

"Oh, I'm sure she says all sorts of stuff." Franny's smile grew a little stiff at that statement.

Mr. Sanchez snorted and turned to sit at the table. Catalina had never managed to think of him as anything other than Mr. Sanchez. As much as his wife welcomed her and insisted she call her Franny, he thought it would be better if Catalina stayed in her part of the world. Which meant the big house.

The knots pulled tighter. She should have warned Willa not to mention her other grandmother. But knowing her daughter, she would ask why. *Please God, help me find a way to blend our families, for my daughter's sake.*

Pulling a mason jar from the cabinet, Franny filled it with water and then arranged the flowers. "Fresh flowers are the best."

"GiGi says the same thing. She's mad that Uncle Trevor told her she can't have them delivered to the house every week. But I'll tell her she can pick them herself."

"Laura Wimberly picking her own flowers. Now that is a sight I'd like to see."

"Jose." Franny glared at him, then shot a meaningful glance at Willa.

Her sweet innocent baby didn't have a clue about the tension in the room. She climbed into the chair next to Andres's father. "Mama said you are the one that really runs the ranch. Longer than I've been alive. Maybe you can show GiGi where they grow, then you could see her picking flowers. I'll come along. It'll be fun."

Jose opened his mouth, but Franny cut him off. What's your favorite breakfast taco?" She moved to the stove."

"I like bean and cheese. Mama likes egg and potato. She said you're the best cook ever. Mama's a good cook, but she said she learned from you because GiGi doesn't cook. I like cooking, though. I help Mama in the kitchen. I'm a good helper."

Not sure where to go, Catalina hovered between the living area and the table. Franny was on the other side of the counter that separated the table from the kitchen.

"Sit. Sit. I'll bring everything to you." Franny tossed another tortilla onto the cast-iron griddle.

Willa had pulled her sketchbook out and was showing her drawings to Mr. Sanchez. "I'm an artist like my mama. She designs games on the phone."

He was acting very impressed. He looked at Catalina with a brow raised.

"I'm a graphic artist for mobile apps. I work for a company based in Canada."

Franny gasped. "Canada? That's so far away." Tears filled her eyes. "Will you be moving there?"

"With my position, I currently can work from home." And that was the truth, for now. She might not even get the new job this go-around.

"You make pictures for phones? That doesn't sound like a real job." Mr. Sanchez, who was more like her father than he would ever realize, didn't see any type of creative endeavor as real work.

She was about to sit next to her daughter when a sound behind her caused her to turn.

Andres stood at the edge of the hallway that led to the bedrooms. His hair was wet. He must have been in the shower when they got here.

"Hi, Andres." She clasped her hands in front of her and tried to steady her heart. He had the power to destroy her world if he wanted to retaliate.

A gasp came from her daughter as her chair slid across the wood floor and she rushed to stand next to Catalina. "Hello. You're him. You're my dad." She stood on her toes and looked as if she was seeing her hero for the very first time.

He approached them, never taking his eyes off Willa. Crouching in front of their daughter, he smiled. "Hello there."

Without warning Willa threw herself at him, causing him to lose his balance. They tumbled to the ground. Franny and Mr. Sanchez rushed over to help. Horrified, Catalina froze. "Willa!"

Surrounded in a cloud of pink tulle, Andres pulled himself up without losing his hold on Willa. His eyes squeezed tight. For a moment everyone was silent. Taking a deep breath, he gazed at Willa with wonder. "I was afraid you'd be shy. I should have known better. Your mother knocked me down the first time I met her."

"I did not." Catalina was quick to defend herself.

"She did?" Willa said at the same time.

Hands on hips, Franny shook her head at them. It was the same look she had used all the time with the kids growing up. "Breakfast is ready. Get off the floor and come sit at the table."

"Sorry," Willa muttered but didn't show any sign of letting him go. "GiGi would be very upset with my overly ex…ex…" She frowned. "Exu-ber-ant greeting." The new word was pronounced very slowly. "You're even better in real life than in a picture."

Andres's forehead wrinkled as he got to

his feet. "Don't ever apologize for being happy to see me. You've seen pictures of me?"

"Yes. You didn't seem as big in the pictures, and your hair was longer. Mama told me all about you. How did she knock you over? Was she excited to see you, too?"

"Oh no. It was the opposite. We...uhm..."

Franny chuckled. "They pretty much hated each other at first sight but then became best friends."

Catalina groaned. She glared at Andres, but he was staring at his mother.

She was going to sound like a brat.

"My father," he continued, "told me to go help the boss's daughter. That's your mom. She was practicing riding sheep for the rodeo, but she made it clear she didn't need my help. The sheep butted her with its head. Knocked her into a mud puddle, on her bottom. Since she told me to go away, I was sitting on the fence watching. I started laughing so hard, I didn't see her coming. No one warned me about her temper. She knocked me off the fence into a patch of bull nettle."

"Oh no. Did you cry?" Willa had had her own run-in with bull nettle once.

"I thought about it just to make her feel bad." He grinned. "It was cold out, so I was pretty well covered with my jacket, gloves and boots. But I made sure to holler a lot."

"Andres Guillermo Sanchez," his mother chided. "You were supposed to help her, not laugh at the poor thing."

"Mom, did you miss the part where she refused my help?" He sounded more like the kid he used to be instead of a grown man. "She said she didn't need some skinny dumb boy to show her how to handle livestock. She was a Wimberly. Seems I've always been an easy target for the Wimberly women." He avoided Catalina's gaze as he kept his focus on Willa. "You're more than welcome to tackle me at any time." He led Willa to the table.

"Your mom did make sure he got home safely." Franny offered a sweet smile. "The poor things were all wet and muddy. She was afraid to go home until she cleaned up. That was the beginning of their relationship. I never could tell if—"

"Mom." Andres shot his mother a hard glare.

Catalina was sure he was thinking the same thing she was. Neither of them would want to unpack their complicated relationship in front of their daughter.

His gaze softened when he looked down at the small hand in his.

The sight left Catalina's heart puddled at the bottom of her gut. It was so unreal to see them together.

"Well, anyway," his mom continued, pulling her out of her thoughts. "After that, I couldn't keep your mom out of our kitchen." Franny smiled at Willa. "I hope it becomes a second home to you, too."

"I saw pictures of y'all when you were

kids like me." She scooted her chair as close to him as she could get.

"Yep." His throat worked. Catalina could tell he was trying to be the calm, steady Andres his family had always relied on. She had relied on him, too.

There was only one time he had allowed strong emotion to take over. It was the night his mother had told him she had cancer. Now the consequence of that night was cuddled up next to him, listening to every word.

"I was seven and she was eight when we officially met." He tried to make his voice sound even, but she knew he was on the verge of losing control of his emotions.

She spooned the beans into a tortilla for Willa and handed it to her. Hopefully, it would give him a minute to collect himself. She couldn't imagine what was running through his head. "What he forgot to mention was I won the next rodeo. And the one after that, too."

Clearing his throat, he blinked and

turned his face away from Willa. "Because you're stubborn and your father told you that you couldn't do it." After filling a tortilla with beans and cheese, he added egg and bacon.

"I want egg and bacon in my taco, Mama." Willa pointed to the bowl of scrambled eggs and the plate of bacon. "That surely blows my mind." She loved using new phrases she heard and picked up from her grandparents. "I've never thought about it before. You just give me bean and cheese."

"Because it's what you like." And yes, she sounded a bit defensive.

Franny sat at the table, tossing more freshly made tortillas into the basket. "You're so precious. I love the way you talk. You can have as much egg and bacon as you want. They are your father's favorites. You will have to spend more time here and we can teach you Spanish. It's important to know as many languages as possible."

"Yo hablo algo de español." Willa's grin matched the brightness in her eyes. *"Este taco es muy bueno.* I said the taco was very good. Did I say it right?"

"Perfecto," Franny replied, then looked to Catalina. "You've taught her Spanish?"

"Don't worry. I know how horrible my accent is. Her preschool has a dual-language program."

Franny frowned. "Preschool? She's so young. How long has she been in school?"

"A little over a year." Her skin tightened. She wasn't used to others questioning her choices for Willa. "My mother was helping me, but Willa is very active and inquisitive. I feared she was spending too much time with adults and needed interaction with children her own age."

Willa nodded. "GiGi said I was a handful and too smart for my britches. I needed pro fish in all help. But I don't really like fish."

"She means professional. My mother was taking care of her while I was at school or working, and she thought Willa needed more than we could give her. She was right. Willa thrives in a structured learning environment. They have a hands-on, play-based philosophy."

"I love school. I learned about the penguins. Then we went to the zoo and saw them. GiGi went with us. She says I'm so smart I could be a scientist."

Andres nodded. "Do you want to be a scientist?"

"I don't know. There are so many things. Maybe a cowboy. PawPaw says the Wimberlys have worked this land for hundreds of years and I might be the last hope to carry on his legs at sea."

Andres's lips moved as he silently tried to figure out the last word. "Legacy."

"I'm a cowboy, and it's hard work," Andres's father said as he reached for another tortilla. "Your dad is a part-time cowboy."

"I thought you were a pilot. Mom told me your dream was to fly airplanes."

"Dreams change as you get older. So

it's okay if you don't know, or even if you change your mind. I did get my pilot's license and fly small planes. Now I fly helicopters more."

"Flying is so cool. PawPaw owns a couple of planes and a helicopter. Have you flown those? He's sick. Uncle Trevor says we have too many and wants to sell some. PawPaw got mad and told him… Well, I didn't really understand what he said, but he was mad."

Catalina put her hand on Willa's arm. "Sweetheart. We talked about eavesdropping."

"They were yelling, Mama. I didn't mean to hear them."

"Yes, well." She avoided making eye contact. "Thank you, Franny, for the delicious breakfast. It brought back so many wonderful memories. I think it's time for us to head back."

Franny's eyes went wide, and her gaze darted to her son. Then she turned back to Catalina with a big smile. She appeared more terrified than happy. "But you just got here. I have…" Her hands waved around the room as if trying to find an excuse for them to stay.

"Uhm. Let me help clean up, and you can talk with Willa. She loves talking." Catalina gathered the empty dishes from the table and gave Willa the floor to charm her new grandparents.

"I do." Willa sat up straighter. "I love talking. GiGi says it's important to not say everything that's in your head. Are you a real cowboy, Buelito? Do you have a horse? Did you know my PawPaw got me my very own horse? He told me about it right before he went to the hospital. It'll be at the ranch soon."

"Is it one of the Wimberly quarter horses?" Andres asked.

"Nope. I told him I wanted a white horse with red polka dots. I saw one in a book and it was so pretty. It took him a while, but he said he found the perfect one for me in Montana. It's not here yet."

Mr. Sanchez leaned back with a frown on his face. "Mr. Wimberly is allowing an Appaloosa on his ranch with his prime quarter horses?"

Catalina chuckled. "Mr. Wimberly and Willa's PawPaw are two completely different people."

"Mama, that does not make any sense." Her daughter frowned at her.

"Do you know how to ride?" Andres asked as he took the leftovers to the counter, then pulled containers out to store them.

"I'm sure I do. PawPaw said Wimberlys are born knowing how to ride." Her forehead and nose scrunched. "But I'm a Sanchez, too. Do you know how to ride?"

Mr. Sanchez looked offended. "Sanchez folks were the best vaqueros in the area before the Wimberlys set foot in this state."

"José!" Franny said between gritted teeth, then smiled and waved at Andres. "Noah will be here soon. He is always starving." She turned to Willa. "Noah is your *tío*. He's my youngest son. You have two aunts, too, Tia Eva and Tia Maya."

As Catalina and Andres washed and dried the pots and pans, Mr. and Mrs. Sanchez talked about their three younger children. Franny showed Willa pictures of Maya, Eva and Noah.

Andres leaned in close as he dried the last skillet she had washed. He was too close. His warmth had as much an impact on her as his fresh masculine scent. With the last dish done, she turned to escape— but a light touch stopped her.

"Cat. We have to talk in private. There are a million questions buzzing around in my head, and Willa doesn't need to hear them."

She didn't want to be anywhere alone with him, but he was right. Talking was inevitable, and stalling wasn't going to fix anything. Hands clasped in front of her, she nodded.

He finally moved away from her, and

she let out the breath she had been holding, steadying herself. Willa was smiling and chatting away.

Andres put his hand on his mother's shoulder. "Cat and I are going to step out back for a moment. Willa, will you keep an eye on my parents?"

She giggled. "I'm a good watcher."

With a few more words, he walked to the back door and held it open, waiting for her. "I thought we'd meet in town later?"

He didn't say anything, just stood there waiting for her to comply. She wasn't ready.

It didn't matter if she was ready or not. She sighed. There was a chance he would never forgive her for this, but they had to make it work for Willa. Catalina didn't want her daughter to be torn between the two families. Between her and Andres.

She missed her best friend, and it was her fault.

The unshed tears burned her throat and eyes. She wanted to cry for everything she had lost, but what she wanted was not what was needed right now. It was time for her to be strong. No tears. She walked through the door.

This was about Andres and his daughter and making it right.

Chapter Four

Andres followed her out, then moved to the edge of the porch and stood with his back to her. There was so much to talk about, so many details to figure out. But all he could think about was the little girl who sat next to him at the table.

Willa had glowed. She had looked at him as if he were her world. How was it possible to love someone without knowing them?

He loved his family, had loved Catalina at one time, but this consumed him in a way that should scare him. It didn't, and yet it did. He had a daughter, and in a split second she had become his world.

He needed to be a part of her daily life. How was he going to take care of her and protect her if he wasn't?

Having Willa in his life meant that he was going to have to deal with Cat every day, too. She had hurt him in more ways than he thought possible.

This time, though, she would not be the one in control. Things would be on his terms. He took in the fresh, crisp air. He'd never take this for granted again. In a distant pasture, cows called out. They were being moved, and normally his dad would be out there, leading the drive. But they had already lost five years with Willa, and José hadn't wanted to miss this first meeting with his only grandchild.

Andres clenched the railing and forced the fire that burned in his gut back to a simmer.

Anger, no matter how justified, wasn't going to get him what he wanted. Strong emotions and loss of self-control never led to anything good. Then the smile of the little girl he'd just met flashed in front of him. His mother loved to say that God could turn any mistake into His good. Willa was proof of that.

He took a deep breath. "First, I need you to understand that I will do anything for Willa, but don't think for a minute that you can flash me that sad smile and get anything you want. I don't think I'll ever be able to forgive you for this. It's more than some stupid stunt. This is my daughter. My *familia*." The last word barely made it past his lips. His throat tightened. "How could you?"

Finally giving in, he took his gaze away from the horizon and turned to her. That was a mistake. Her large eyes were brimming with unshed tears. He bit down hard with his back molars, stopping the softening of his heart.

Her teeth bit her bottom lip, and she

ducked her head, breaking eye contact. Before looking up, she wiped at her face.

She leaned forward in the rocking chair and met his gaze, holding it. "You have no reason to trust me, but I promise I'm here to help build a bond between you and Willa. There is no question that you will be the best father. I'm sorry I wasn't strong enough sooner."

Chewing on that bottom lip, she closed her eyes for a brief moment. Then she lifted her chin and gave him that sad smile he had just told her wouldn't work on him any longer.

"It might put your mind at rest to know that I've been working with a counselor at my church. I can't go on blaming my parents for my poor decisions. I have to take ownership if my life is going to move forward."

His jaw hurt. Relaxing, he put his weight on the railing behind him. "Why? Your parents were horrible. I'm not sure they deserve forgiveness."

She shook her head. "But I can't let their mistakes hold me back from everything I can be in Christ. I was so tired of anger coloring my life and of trying to prove that I didn't care, when I did. Very much. All I wanted was for them to love me and not see me as the mistake."

She turned to stare out over the ranch. "Your parents are closer in age to my sister and brother. My parents thought they were done and had moved on with their lives. They weren't prepared for me. No one was prepared for me. Other than you. But then I…"

Her fingers twisted in her lap. "Speaking of parents, how did yours take the news?" She looked over her shoulder as if she could see through the walls.

"They were shocked, furious and elated." From the minute he had pulled his parents out of bed last night and broken the news, his father had glared at him as though this injustice was all his fault.

Andres sighed and rubbed his hand on the back of his neck.

In some ways it was, but he couldn't take responsibility for something he didn't know about. But he hadn't been strong enough in his pushback to the Wimberlys. He had walked away just like her when the wall seemed too high to climb. He should have found a rope, or dug a tunnel, anything to learn why she had held him that night, then left.

He shut his eyes against the headache that had been pushing at his skull for the last twelve hours. Shock, guilt and anger still warred in his brain.

"Last night my father yelled for a full hour. My father. He never yells. My mother tried to calm him, but then he yelled at her. That stopped him cold."

"He was mad at *you*?" Confusion marked her expression.

It wouldn't do any good to repeat his father's words. *You got Wimberly's daughter pregnant? How stupid can you be? This is not how I raised you.* He had never done anything to disappoint his father, and it had hurt.

"Sometime after midnight, my mother curled up next to Papá and hugged him. She whispered that they had a grand-daughter." He shook his head. They had melted into each other right there in his father's old recliner. "My father nodded with that crooked grin of his. He looked at me and demanded to know when they would get to meet her." He pointed to the house. "Now they're all in and over the moon about her."

Last night, the idea of Willa had been in the abstract. After seeing her, his daugh-ter, awe was shifting his heart in ways he couldn't have anticipated. He was hav-ing a hard time believing that she was sitting at the table chatting with his par-ents. His daughter, Willemina Francisca Wimberly.

In that moment, his life was changed forever. He had never understood love at first sight. He definitely didn't believe in it. But then he saw Willa.

Yeah. That was love on such a deep level that it blew the walls off everything he had experienced before.

His gaze scanned the wide horizon of the ranch, seeking answers he still didn't have. The first time Catalina had come out to the ranch, he had seen her from a distance. She had been about the same age their daughter was now. He had thought she was a real princess.

A grin pulled at the corner of his mouth. Once he had met her, that notion had been crushed. She was nothing like he imagined a princess would be. Other than bossy. She'd always had something to say and was constantly ready for a battle.

A soft touch pulled him out of his musings. He looked at Cat.

Her features had softened. Was it hope? "What's the grin for?" she asked.

"Nothing." He looked back through the kitchen window. "She's beautiful."

"You won't get an argument from me. There's so much of you and your family in her. She's supersmart, so much smarter than me—which was a huge relief to my parents. But she also has the biggest heart and loves school. That's all you."

He frowned. "You're smart."

"You were the only one who thought so." Shaking her head, she snorted and looked through the same window. "More like a smart-mouthed brat."

"Cat." He hated it when she put herself down. He heard Mr. Wimberly in each bitter word.

"Sorry. Old habits and all. I don't see any signs of a learning disability, but she is young. Of course, my sister and brother don't have any either, so the odds are in her favor that my ADD and dyslexia skipped her."

He wanted to hang on to the anger a little longer. He had every right. But he also was very much aware of the hurts she kept buried away from public view.

There had always been so much more to her than people saw. Than even she saw.

"There is nothing wrong with wanting to be your own person and fighting for what you want when others are telling you what they think you should do." That was one of the traits he had admired about her, even though she went about it the wrong way most of the time.

She was standing next to him now, her arms braced on the railing as she studied the far-reaching pastures of the Wimberly Cattle Company.

"You always talked about flying." Her voice was low and soft, as if she was afraid of scaring him off. "What happened to your dreams of being a pilot in the air force?"

He sighed. The only problem was those had never truly been his dreams. Just as she tended to do the opposite of what people told her to do, he had a hard time saying no to the expectations of others. Because he was good in school, top of his class and he wanted to fly, everyone, including his parents, thought the air force was the perfect career path for him.

Mr. Wimberly had helped his family get him into the prep school. The academy was the next step. Everyone was so proud of him.

"With Mom's treatments taking their toll, they needed more help here at home." For some reason he didn't want her to know that it had been a relief to come home. He had never wanted to join the air force. The guilt that he had had any type of personal benefit from his mother's illness ate at him.

"Your family has been through so much. I'm sorry I added to it. But at the time, I truly thought I was protecting your mom."

As much trouble as Cat got into, she never had done anything to hurt anyone. He was close enough to put an arm around her. But he wouldn't allow himself to go there.

If his reactions followed the same old

pattern, he'd forgive her soon. He gritted his teeth. He didn't want to go soft. This time she had gone too far. There would be no going back to an easy friendship. Walking down the steps, he picked up a stray rock and chunked it over the fence.

Stay focused, he chided himself. "What's next? How do you see us moving forward?"

Using the back of her long sleeve, Catalina wiped at her face, then stepped closer to the window. "I'm not sure." She peeked inside before moving to the steps and sitting down. "I've always imagined her here in your family's kitchen. Sitting at the table chatting with your parents. It seemed so natural. My best memories happened there."

"Then why stay away for so long? Why keep her from us? Was it your father? He didn't want anyone to know his granddaughter was a Sanchez?" Rage flared. Heat climbed his neck. He never had a problem with his emotions taking control, but he had to hold himself back from hitting the side of the house. His fingers tightened on the railing.

Not realizing the battle that waged inside him, she sighed and crossed her arms over her knees. "It was me. Not meeting the expectations of the Wimberly legacy and such."

There was no way he could miss the longing in her eyes. What was she thinking? He had never been sure. And her moods had always changed faster than the Texas weather.

"I wasn't following the plan." She finally broke the long silence. "According to him, my selfishness would ruin your future."

"What?" He hadn't expected that.

Her laughter was rough and harsh. "The rare times my father was home for dinner, you were held up as the shining example of hard work, brains and ambition. Everything my brother and I didn't have, even though we had all the advantages. Apparently, my brother and I are completely useless. At times, he seemed to forget that he still had Krystal. The perfect Wimberly who made past generations proud. Of course, she's too busy and important to ever come home. At the time, I thought he loved her more. I didn't realize their relationship was just as dysfunctional."

Krystal and Trevor had already been in their teens when Catalina had come along. The two older Wimberly kids had as much in common as West Texas had with East Texas. He dropped his head.

The Wimberly family had issues. Andres's father was always warning him and his siblings just to do the work they were hired for and not get personally involved with the family.

But he had never known anyone who needed a friend more than Catalina Wimberly. Now his daughter was part of that family drama that her parents called legacy.

His daughter was so young and innocent. The thought of any of them making her feel useless the way they had done to Cat tore at him. He had to find a way to protect her.

"I want her to stay with me. With my parents when I'm working. We have a lot of time to make up. I also want my name on her birth certificate. I'll pay for the DNA test and court fees. Whatever is required."

Panic flared in her eyes. "You want to take her from me?" Her gaze darted to their daughter inside. She jumped from the step and spun around. His hand circled her upper arm to stop her. His fingers slipped gently down to hers.

"No. That's not what I meant. You were so lonely in that house. I hated that they made you feel worthless. How could you want our daughter to live there?"

She was facing away from him, refusing to make eye contact. "We don't live here. I moved her to Austin. What about you? You were top of your class and had so much going for you. Even if you didn't go to the Air Force Academy, you had other options. Growing up, all you talked about was flying around the world." She turned to look over his shoulder. Tears filled her eyes, but she blinked until they were pushed back. "Why are you still here?"

"When my mother got sick and you left, I learned I wanted a different life than I imagined. This is not about me, Catalina."

He put one hand on her shoulder and the other under her chin and waited for her to meet his gaze.

"She's yours, and she obviously adores you as much as you adore her. But I need a chance to get to know her. To be a real father to her." His throat closed for a moment. For the last five years, his daughter had been in the world, and he had been walking around without a clue.

He needed to make sure she was as well-adjusted as Cat told him she was. The drive to protect her from the Wimberly family was overwhelming. "I have a house in town. There's an extra bedroom we can set up for her. Or I can move back here to be closer to her if that would make it easier. I'll give you my work schedule so we can work around that. But my parents deserve to know her as well as your parents do. How long will you be here?"

Her body posture softened. "I'm not sure. My work can be done from anywhere. My mom helped me set up a studio in one of the extra bedrooms at the big house." She crossed her arms and looked at him. "The heart attack has given my father a true scare. I'm here to support Mom the way she supported me."

"I'm sorry about your father, but the house has to be full of stress. Maybe it would be better for everyone for Willa to move in with me."

Her eyes went wide, and she moved closer to him. "You want full custody because my father is ill?"

"No." His hands went to her upper arms

and he looked directly into her eyes. "I just want to be with her as much as possible while you are here. And maybe it'll help you, too."

Lips in a tight line, she stepped away from him. "That's one reason I'm here. But I can't allow you to uproot her. She wouldn't understand being away from me. My daughter has never had a moment to feel unwanted or abandoned."

"Our daughter."

The starch went out of her stance and she sat down on the porch swing. "Andres, she's never spent the night away from me. Most of the time, she sleeps in my room. Until she started preschool this year, it was me, my parents and her. That's it. That's her world. You can't expect me to just turn her over to you and walk away."

"I'm not asking you to leave her. I just want to spend real time with her and my parents. What did you think would happen when you showed up with my daughter in tow? You know how important family is to us."

He turned his back to her and braced his hands on the beam over his head, looking out at the Wimberly ranch. His family had always worked the land, but her family owned it. His daughter owned it. "Your family should have loved and protected you, and we both know it didn't happen that way. You came to my family home to find a safe place. Why wouldn't you want the same for Willa?"

"I was born obstinate, a rebel without a cause. It was instinct for me to do and be the opposite of what they wanted. That, coupled with my ADD and dyslexia, meant that they were clueless as to how to handle me. She's so different."

He whipped around and pointed at her. "Don't you dare take the blame for their lousy parenting. They tore you down because you didn't fit the perfect Wimberly mold. I won't stand by and let them pass that legacy on to *my* daughter." Everything that had been coiled since she'd told him about Willa sprang free. "I will fight to protect her. Whatever it takes to keep her safe, consider it done. If I have to get a lawyer—"

Catalina was standing in front of him before he finished. She pressed her hand against his heart. "Andres. I don't want to fight you. My parents are so different with her. Plus, I set ground rules. Your family showed me how a home should always be the safe place in this chaotic world. If anyone tries to tell her how to be a Wimberly, they lose time with her. I promise, as grandparents, they are everything I wanted in my parents."

He had a hard time imagining Mr. and Mrs. Wimberly as fun-loving grandparents.

"Andres, I know this is hard for you to understand, and I'm so sorry. How about we plan some sleepovers? I'm sure as a deputy you have a crazy work schedule. Her birthday is the end of the week before Thanksgiving. I was thinking we could plan a party on neutral territory. Your mom and mine could both help. Somewhere in town. And there's the holidays. We can do all the Christmas stuff together. I promise, I want you and your family in her life."

"You think we can do everything together? Your family and mine?" He stuffed his hands in his pockets. "Are your parents going to cause problems?"

"No. My father's on board." Tears welled up again. "His heart is not doing well. All the things he thought were important..." She shrugged. "Well, they got realigned. My mom just found out that you're Willa's father last night, but don't worry about her. She loves Willa and wants the best for her."

"She really didn't notice that her granddaughter looks like a Sanchez?"

"She's good at not seeing anything that could create an uncomfortable situation. So she looks past what she doesn't want to know and doesn't ask questions. I'm the one making the decision about Willa. You and me. We're her parents. It's between us and no one else."

He didn't say a word, but he made sure to give her the look. The one that told her he didn't for one moment, believe that Laura Wimberly was going to be a pushover or think that the Sanchez family had anything to offer a Wimberly.

"Andres. They'll do what's best for Willa. I'll make sure. We'll be on the ranch through the holidays."

She bit down on her lip and cut her gaze to the pastures surrounding the house. "No matter what happens, the earliest we'll leave is January. That gives us two months. My personal goal is for you to have a strong relationship with her before we return home. I want you to share in as much as we can. We can be good coparents."

He wanted to yell that two months was not enough when he had already lost five years. Port Del Mar should be her home. There had to be a way to keep them here. Austin was six hours away. How did co-parenting happen so far apart? How could he protect her?

He needed her to understand how important this was to him and his family. Andres said calmly, "Cat, the best moments in life are the small pieces of time between the big events. Getting ready for the day, making dinner, watching a movie on the sofa. Waking up late on days off and making pancakes in pajamas. Bedtime prayers. Those are the memories that bond my family. How can I have those with Willa if she's six hours away?" Every muscle in his body tightened as he waited for her response.

"We'll get creative. There are lots of happy kids who live between two families."

"I don't want to be an every-other-weekend dad." That was straight out of his nightmares.

The door opened. His mother fisted her apron. There was a deep unease in the brown depths of her eyes.

"Mom?" Moving to her, he gently placed his hand on her shoulder. "What's wrong?"

Her smile was tight. "Nothing, *mijo*. Mrs. Wimberly is here. She came for a visit. Isn't that nice?"

Chapter Five

"My mother's here?" Catalina closed her eyes and tilted her head all the way back. Her lips moved as if saying a silent prayer.

"It's okay, Mom." Andres kissed his mother on the cheek as he walked past her and into the house. This might be Mrs. Wimberly's ranch, but this was his mother's kitchen, and no one was going to come into it and upset her.

Catalina slipped under his arm as he opened the door. She looked over her shoulder with an unspoken plea. She wanted him to play nice after she had just promised that her mother wouldn't be a problem. Was she delusional or just outright lying to him?

Not once in over two decades had any of Catalina's family set foot in his parents' house. Now Laura Wimberly needed to stop by to say hi?

In the sunny kitchen, Mrs. Wimberly was sitting on the edge of a farm chair. Her back stiff, she had her fingers, decorated with several rings, folded on the table and a huge fake smile on her perfectly painted red lips. She wore a black turtleneck with a short, fitted turquoise jacket. As always, she had an exquisite large handcrafted silver-and-turquoise cross hanging around her neck. She must have had over a hundred of them. This was her casual look.

"Mama! Look—GiGi came. I told you she wanted to visit, too." Willa stood next to her grandmother, but her smile was genuine.

"I see that." Cat's jaw was tight. "Mom? What are you doing? We agreed Willa would spend time with the Sanchez family without you."

"I know that, sweetheart. But I was about to go to town and your visit was going so long I thought I'd stop by to make sure everything was good. This is all new to our baby, and I don't want her scared or overwhelmed."

Andres crossed his arms. "We aren't the ones who overwhelm or intimidate people."

His mother swatted at him. "Andres." The warning was said for his ears only. With a welcoming gesture, she turned back to Mrs. Wimberly. "Let me get you some coffee."

"It's been wonderful, GiGi." Willa went on to explain in detail everything they had done. His mother set a cup of coffee in front of Mrs. Wimberly.

"Thank you, Francisca." Her eyes went wide, then narrowed on Catalina. "Willemina Francisca. She's named after them."

"It's cool, isn't it, GiGi?" The child bounced and clapped. "My daddy's middle name is Guillermo. That's why Mama named me Willemina."

All the adults quieted. Andres wanted to tell her to get out of their house, but not only would his mother faint in horror over his rudeness, Willa wouldn't understand. So he stayed quiet and stood still, but on guard, ready to intervene.

His father pushed away from the table. "It's time I got back to work."

Mrs. Wimberly nodded, as if giving him permission. "We're moving the north herd today, correct? How many will we be taking to market?"

"I apologize, Mrs. Wimberly. But we have a rule never to bring business talk to our family table. I'll be at the big house tomorrow at 8:00 a.m. to give you and Trevor an update." Jose grabbed his hat off the hook and headed for the door. Andres gave him a knowing look. They talked about the ranch at the table all the time. His father, who never lied, had just lied.

"Buelito!" Willa ran after him. "We have to hug and kiss goodbye."

His stoic father turned and dropped to one knee. The corners of his mouth turned up. "Of course, *mija*. I'm new to being a buelito. You will have to be patient and forgive me." Arms out, he welcomed her. Running into them, she laughed and kissed his cheek.

"It's okay. Love you!" She squeezed her arm around his neck and gave him another loud smack on his cheek. His mother had her hands clasped over her heart and misty tears in her eyes.

Mrs. Wimberly was staring at her coffee cup with an intensity the coffee shouldn't have inspired. "May I have sugar and cream?"

"Of course, Mrs. Wimberly." Franny, who was hovering by the table, turned to the kitchen. Andres stepped forward to stop her, but Catalina cut him off.

"Mother, this is their time to spend with Willa. They are not here to serve you."

"Oh no..." his mother started, but he pulled out a chair for her. Cat smiled and nodded to the chair, encouraging his mother to sit.

Once both women were settled back into their farm chairs, Cat grabbed the sugar bowl and spoon, then came back to the table with the coffeepot. "Franny, please sit. Here, take this cup of coffee."

"Oh, I couldn't," his mother protested, but Cat poured the coffee anyway, then sat.

Willa came back to the table once his father had left the house. She climbed into Mrs. Wimberly's lap. "GiGi. I had the best breakfast tacos today. Buelita made them. Even the tortillas. Did you know they start as little round balls of dough? Can I drink coffee?"

Since standing and staring had not chased Cat's mother away, Andres grabbed a cup and joined them at the table. His mother stood again. "I'll get you some chocolate milk, *mija*."

Cat was faster. "Please sit. I'll get her drink."

"But she doesn't drink chocolate milk," Cat's mother protested, with a sharp edge to her voice.

"I've never had it. It sounds delicious." Willa clapped. "Two of my favorite things. Chocolate and milk."

"But it has tons of sugar."

Willa frowned. "But GiGi, you just put two big spoonfuls of sugar in your coffee."

Franny covered her mouth to hide her giggle. Andres had to smile, too.

Mrs. Wimberly sighed. "This is true." She sipped her coffee. "But I am fully grown."

Cat came back with two glasses that had previously been jelly jars. "Here you go. I'm going to drink chocolate milk, too. I haven't had it in years. It was always my favorite."

"You didn't drink it as a child." Her mother frowned. "I don't remember your favorite drink."

"I drank it here. Franny always had it. It was Noah's favorite, too." Everyone focused on their drinks. "Mother, isn't it time for you to go to town?"

"Why?" Willa pouted. "I want everyone together."

"Not today, sweetheart." Mrs. Wimberly kissed her on the top of her head, then placed her in the chair to her left. Standing, she adjusted her fitted jacket. "Your mother's right. I need to get to town. We can have a tea party another time."

She jumped up. "Yay! I know! Daddy, Buelita and Buelito can come too. You'll come, won't you, Buelita?"

Andres's mother's eyes went wide, and she blinked several times before looking at him with panic in her eyes.

Cat reached across the table. "Not today, sweetheart."

"But why not? We can have it at the fancy table. It's so big. That'd be fun."

Her mother frowned. "Willa. Your

mother said no. It's impolite to argue with her in front of others."

"These aren't others, GiGi. They're family. You and Uncle Trevor fight all the time in front of family."

Andres wanted to cheer his daughter for standing up to her grandmother, but making an enemy out of Mrs. Wimberly this early would not help him.

He leaned forward. "We have lots of time to figure this all out. You can spend the rest of the morning here and have lunch with my brother and sisters. When your GiGi gets home, you can have tea with her." He glanced at his mother. She had tears in her eyes but a smile on her face.

"Yes, *mija*, that's a wonderful idea. Your daddy is a very smart man."

Willa sighed. "Okay. But I don't understand why we can't all be together."

This time Cat's mother bent down to talk to Willa. "When mommies and daddies aren't married, they have to take turns and share. I know you've always been with us, but things are different now."

"Then Mama and Daddy should get married. We can all be together then. Your house is so big. We could all live there."

Cat gasped. Andres choked on his coffee. He couldn't even look his mother's way. The whole idea of him having a child without marriage already upset her strong sense of right and wrong.

"It's not that simple. And it doesn't work that way." Who knew Mrs. Wimberly would be the reasonable one? She gave Willa a hug. "I'll see you back at home. As a special treat, I'll pick up the fancy cookies at the bakery you love. Today you'll get to eat them fresh since I don't have to drive them to Austin."

"Thank you, GiGi! How about my birthday party? We can all be together then, right? I want to have a fancy tea party and dance like a princess. Maybe my birthday wish will be for Mama and Daddy to get married."

"Oh, sweetheart. I think it's too late for that one. But we can find a way to all be there for you." She looked at his mother. "We can, right?"

His mother nodded. "Yes. I wouldn't miss it."

"Can we have a tea party with dancing fairies at the big table?"

Andres knew there was no way his parents could truly relax and enjoy the first birthday they would have with Willa if it was at the big house. "You know where else fairies like to hang out?"

"In the forest?"

"Yes, and on pirate ships. I happen to have a friend that owns one."

Her eyes were so round they were impossibly big. "You know a pirate?"

"I do, and he loves to have parties on his ship. Would you want to have your party there?"

"Yes! Yes!" She launched herself from the chair and had her arms around his neck before he could blink. "You are the best daddy in the world!"

He was in trouble. There was no way he would ever be able to tell her no or not do everything in his power to make her smile just like this.

Cat's mother smiled at him, and it even looked like a real one. "That is a perfect solution. Mr. Wimberly won't be able to make it, but he has his own surprise for our princess. Well done, Andres. Y'all have a good day." She paused at the door and looked at them over her shoulder as if she were leaving Willa forever. With a quick nod, she left.

His mother visibly relaxed. "It looks as if you've finished your milk. You liked it?"

"Delicious. What can we do now?"

"Do you want to see my garden? Since it's getting colder, we need to pick everything we can. The carrots should be ready. We can use them for lunch, then we can make cookies. How does that sound?"

"You grow your own carrots? I love carrot and raisin salad." She held her hand out to him. "Come on, Daddy." Then she turned to Cat and offered her other hand. "You, too, Mama. We're going to pull carrots out of the ground. This is the best day ever!" She led them out the door behind his humming mother. Outside, she skipped, pulling them along behind her.

His mother gathered two of her baskets off the cedar fence post and held one out for Willa. Dropping their hands, she rushed to her grandmother, then went through the garden gate. He couldn't hear her chatter, but his mother laughed at something his daughter said. Cat gave him a tentative smile, then joined them. His heart ached.

This was the mental picture he had always had of his future family. At one time, his imaginings had included Cat, but he'd learned that was impossible. What was he supposed to do now that he knew she could never be truly his, but they had a daughter?

And in a few months, she would take

Willa to Austin, and he would lose them all over again.

He thought he had put Catalina's abandonment behind him. But apparently his heart was still raw below the surface. Had he been harboring a secret hope that she would come back to him? And what would happen to that spark of hope when she left with Willa again? Would his heart survive?

She'd never stayed in one place or committed to one project for too long, and the one thing he had learned about himself in the last five years was that he wanted deep family roots. Roots he wanted to give his daughter. He had wanted to give them to Cat, but she had cut them and flown away.

What scared him the most was the tender feeling he'd had when he saw her in his mother's kitchen again. For a brief moment he knew she was where she belonged. But that was a lie and he couldn't fall for it again.

For his daughter's sake, he'd find a way

to deal. He had been taught to stay the course no matter what, that you did what people expected of you.

But that was not Cat's world. He had no doubt that when she left this time, she'd be taking what was left of his heart. Maybe he needed to look for work in Austin. The idea turned his stomach, but he couldn't be six hours away from his daughter.

Yesterday, if anyone had asked him to describe the worst moment in his life, he would have gone straight to the January night six years ago when his mother had given him the news that she had been diagnosed with cancer. Catalina Wimberly had been there for him that night. Then she had used him and walked away.

That night had turned into the worst year of his life. Christmas had dimmed. He had lost all the joy the season used to bring. *Humbug* had become his heart's carol. This Christmas, he had a reason to celebrate. He had a daughter. But if he lost her...

There would be no coming back from that darkness. Once again, the mighty Wimberlys had left him with little control of his own life. But for his daughter's sake, he would do whatever it took to bring the joy back.

Monday, he'd be calling a lawyer. He had to find a way to protect his daughter and his heart.

Chapter Six

Despite the cool weather, Catalina's skin was sticky. She tended to overheat when she was anxious. She had played peacemaker as Andres's sisters and mother had worked with her mother to plan Willa's sixth birthday party. Everyone had been polite, but now it was the moment of truth. In thirty minutes, people would be arriving on the faux pirate ship.

Some people she knew well. Others she had just met at church, parents of children in Willa's Sunday school class.

"Daddy!"

She jumped at her daughter's loud

screech. Willa ran past her to tackle him. Her wings fluttered. In her hand was an extra pair of delicate wings she had been saving for him. Catalina grinned. He had no idea of Willa's plan for him.

He held a tall white box high over his head. "Easy, ladybug. I've been tasked with the delivery of one princess cake."

"I want to see! Buelita told me it had a real doll in the middle." Arms still wrapped around Andres's leg, she looked to her mother. "She made them for Tia Maya and Tia Eva every year till they turned fifteen and had a quinceañera. I want a quinceañera." She let go of him and twirled.

He laughed. "My parents will not let you skip that milestone. But we have a few years before you turn fifteen. Love the wings, by the way."

"These are yours!" She stepped back and waved the glittered tulle wings. "I got you the bigger one because you're so big.

You're bigger than Buelito, Tío Noah and Uncle Trevor."

"Yes, I am." The male pride made her smile. "They have to wear wings, too?"

"Everyone has wings."

He laughed and leaned closer to Catalina. "And I was afraid this would be boring. It might be the most entertaining party I've been to in years." With a quick motion, he put space between them and frowned. "Where do I put the cake?"

"The serving area is over here." Together with Willa's help, they set up the party snacks and drinks. "My mom is on the way with the party favors."

"Great." He nodded with a grin and shook the wings at her. "My mom is bringing the piñata."

She had known he'd be the best kind of father, but seeing it tore at her heart. They stood next to each other as Willa skipped around, flittering among the crew and charming them with her questions.

His whole family, including a few cousins, came up the plank, their arms loaded with colorful gifts and party favors. They took over the ship. Paper banners were strung up and Willa laughed as younger cousins were introduced. Her mother and brother joined them. Trevor was carrying a large wooden chest. "We brought the family tea set."

Mrs. Wimberly scanned the deck. "Where will they be serving?"

Captain Carlos took Catalina's mother to the table so she could set it up for the children. Trevor gave Andres a nod as he passed by, but he looked as if he wanted to be anywhere but here.

Andres's whole family, on the other hand, acted as if this was the social event of the year. They were on the other end of the deck. The bright-colored papier-mâché star with ribbons hanging from each point was hoisted into the air, ready to be plundered for its treasures.

He tilted his head. "I think our families have turned it into a competition."

She paused in mixing the fruit juice. "You think? If we're not careful, our daughter will be so spoiled that it will be hard to live with her."

Had she realized how easily she'd said "our daughter"? It was the first time that it had sounded so natural. They were Willa's parents. They were responsible for her, together.

As his sisters, each wearing fairy wings, pulled out more prizes and gifts, he grew a little worried. "How do we stop them?"

"I'm not sure," she whispered back. "With my mom I've always set limits, but now with your family in the mix I think she might be feeling insecure. A Laura Wimberly who doubts her place is a very dangerous creature. I don't have the heart to tell your mom and sisters to back off. You'll have to do that."

"Me? You want me to tell my mother and sisters. And you really think that will work?"

She sighed. "No." Her bottom lip disappeared between her teeth. "So, you're afraid of the women in your family. My mother is afraid of them, too, so that leaves me—"

"Wait. Your mother is afraid of the Sanchez women?" The expression in his eyes told her exactly what he thought. She had lost her mind.

Cat nodded. "She's never had to share Willa with anyone. Your family is so great. Willa loves them already. They're all she talks about. Look." She waved to his family. "She's laughing and dancing with them."

He scoffed. "My sisters are always dancing and singing."

"Exactly. My mom can't compete with that." Glancing over at her mother, she nudged him. "See."

Her mother stood alone, a teacup in hand, looking at the mini party happening on the other end of the deck. The teacup made a soft clicking noise against the saucer. The delicate hand covered in silver jewelry trembled.

Next to her, Andres shook his head. "I never in a million years thought I'd feel sorry for Laura Wimberly."

"At the house she had Willa all excited about using a real tea set. It's a family heirloom. I was never allowed to touch it, let alone use it at a party."

Willa turned just as Andres took a step her way. Her eyes lit up when she saw Cat's mother. "GiGi! You brought the family teacups!" Willa pulled her buelita's and tías' attention along with her as she skipped across the deck. "I told them all about it."

Franny looped an arm through his as she peered at the delicate china. "You have a real tea set for a child's party?"

"She wants a tea party. To serve tea, you need a tea set." Laura smiled. "What use is it if we never pull it out?"

With a huge smile, Willa ran to her grandmother, not stopping until she had wrapped herself around her. "Thank you, GiGi." Then she danced to Andres and Cat and hugged them. "This is going to be the best day ever. Daddy, you have to put on your wings." With that, she skipped back to her grandmothers and aunts, where they now stood talking about the party plans.

He looked at the gathering with concern. "I don't even know where to start."

She laughed and took the wings. "Turn around." He did as she commanded. Slipping the left band up his arm, she made adjustments at his shoulder, then coming around to his front she worked on the right side. "You're taller and broader than you were six years ago."

A groan slipped past her teeth. Why did she say that? Why did she even notice? Heat flared under her skin and her fingers fumbled with the loops.

"I got it." He stepped back. Of course, he did. He couldn't get away from her fast enough. They had been getting along.

Why did she have to go and make it awkward? That was her specialty.

More guests arrived, and the party kept her mind from going into a spiral of self-loathing for making that stupid blunder.

The children had finished their tea, all acting like perfect ladies and gentlemen. Music started as Cat was helping some of the pirate crew put away the china. To her amazement, the delicate pieces were still free of any scratches or chips.

"I want to be a dancer!" Willa twirled in front of her GiGi. All the little girls joined her, along with a few of the boys.

Catalina tensed, waiting for her mother to shut down the idea.

"You know your mother was a dancer. She spent so much time practicing. She would leap and flow around the house. She loved dance."

"Really? Mama, is it true you danced?"

Holding the piñata stick, Andres came up behind the group. "Your mother was the most beautiful dancer. I could watch her for hours." He placed the ribbon-covered stick on the cleared table. "You know I helped her practice."

"You did?"

He nodded, then grabbed Willa and tossed her in the air. "Yes. I would lift her high above my head and she would reach to the sky."

Willa squealed. "Higher, Daddy!"

He laughed and tucked her under his arm. The other children gathered close. "My mama is a dancer!" she yelled at the other children who had moved to Andres. "Daddy would toss her up."

"I would lift her," he said with a wink. "No tossing allowed."

"You should show them some of your moves," her mother encouraged her. "You were so graceful."

Catalina was speechless. The little ones around her pulled her from her frozen state as they cheered in excitement and clapped. "Show us!"

"Can you teach us a dance? I wanted to be a dancer, but the lessons are too far away." The little dark-haired girl with curls had reached out to touch her hand.

Katy, a sweet girl who had hung back earlier, moved forward. "I was in dance lessons over the bridge, but they don't have room for me anymore. I couldn't keep up. Do you think you could teach me?"

The sadness in her sweet face tore at her heart. Katy had braces on her legs. Catalina knew that many dance studios wouldn't accept children who were different or considered difficult.

"Please, Ms. Wimberly. Can you show us how to do a dance?"

"I haven't danced in years."

Her mother smiled. "You taught dance to little ones back in high school. How fun would it be to teach the girls some of your old moves?"

"I want to learn a dance," one of the few boys chimed in.

"And the boys, too," her mother encouraged. Her mother.

Catalina stared at her for a moment. Who was that woman? Not once in all the years she had fought to stay in dance did her mother utter a supportive word. Now she wanted her to teach Willa and her friends a routine.

No time to unpack those feelings and thoughts. She looked at the happy faces watching her. They wanted to dance. For some unexplained reason, her throat tightened from emotions buried long ago.

Her father had taken dance from her, and now her daughter and mother were telling her to dance again. "Okay. Teatime is over. So we'll do a little dance, and then we'll hit the piñata. Get in two lines and stretch your arms out to make sure you have enough space to move."

"Me, too?" Katy was standing to the side.

Before she could tell her *yes*, Willa grabbed the little girl's hand and pulled her into the front line with her. "My mom will teach you."

A couple of the other moms helped the eight children make two rows. The precious little faces were so eager. They looked at her as if she could open a door to a whole new world. They trusted her.

One deep breath. "Ready?"

They all nodded.

"Lift your arms high and point to the east and west with your fingers." She showed them, then waited. "Now, stretch them as far as they can go, then roar like a lion!"

All eight children did exactly as she asked.

"That's not dancing," one of the boys challenged her.

"Maybe not traditional dancing, but it warms up our insides and outsides and reminds us to stand proud like a lion. Now, straighten your spine, shoulders back and head high. Bring your arms around to the front of you, like holding a beach ball. Perfect.

"Lift it over your head."

"We're pirate fairies, so I'm holding a big basket of treasures," Katy said with a huge smile.

"I love it!" Catalina's heart soared at the joy of the children's dance as she took them through several moves.

"Can Daddy catch me?"

She took in the other fathers who were standing around, all friends of Andres's. They were all big, outdoorsy men wearing different shades of sheer fairy wings. Her heart melted. These were tough guys, but they were daddies first.

She couldn't even imagine having this kind of childhood. They were so supportive of their children's creative play. That gave her an idea.

Elijah De La Rosa, the owner of the ship, was standing next to Margarite's husband. "We have several strong dads here. Maybe they can join us, and everyone can do a lift?"

The children dropped their imaginary

treasures and begged their dads to join them. With a few nudges and good-humored jabbing, four men, including Andres, stepped forward. They stood facing the kids. "Back row first," Catalina called. The kids ran to the dads and were lifted high, then held for a minute so that they could pose. "Now down and run back to your places. Front row come forward."

They did it a few more times, with each leap getting bolder. It was the most precious thing she had ever seen.

The kids and adults laughed and cheered, encouraging each other. "I think we can call that a wrap. Everyone take a bow." She showed the children how to sweep down in a graceful bow. They attempted it, but *grace* was not a word she would use to describe her group of ragtag dancers. More along the lines of adorable and beautiful. She turned to the dads. "Take a bow."

Grinning, they did—with not much more grace than the kids.

"Piñata time!" Franny announced. Cat's mother moved in and helped herd the little ones to the other end of the deck.

Before she could follow, a hesitant touch stopped her. Turning, she saw one of the mothers standing there. "Hi. I'm Carol. Katy's mom. We met at church. I wanted to thank you for including Katy in the party. It's all she talked about this week. You did a great job teaching on the fly like that. I was wondering if you did private lessons."

"Oh. I don't know."

"Katy is so sweet and listens really well. But she can't always keep up and..." She paused. "Well, sometimes people see her and are afraid of working with her. She loves dance so much. I know she's not very coordinated."

Her words rushed on, stumbling over themselves. "I told her it was too far to drive, but they told me they were not trained to handle special needs. Which is ridiculous. If they knew Katy, they would know she's like every other little girl."

Carol blinked a few times. "I'm sorry to ramble. You were just so good with all the kids. And you pulled the dads in. I'm a single mom. Edward left when... Well, her dad is not in the picture." She looked away as if she was embarrassed. "I couldn't pay much. I'm sorry." She looked back at Catalina. "Forget I said anything. They just had so much fun."

"It's okay. I'm a single mom, too. I think it was fun for all of us." She glanced at Andres, who was helping the kids aim the stick to hit the colorful star full of goodies. She wasn't alone anymore when it came to raising Willa. "I haven't taught in years, but we could do a weekly playdate with some dancing. Willa would love that. No fees. I do need to find a place where we can meet. I don't think a pirate ship would be very practical."

"I can ask around. The church has a youth center. It even has a little stage."

Bella, one of the De La Rosa siblings her mother wouldn't let her hang out with when she was a kid, joined the conversation. "I would love to have a dance group here. With four girls it gets expensive at the studio over the bridge, and I don't care for their attitudes. I would love to have something close. My girls don't have dreams of being world-renowned dancers. They just like to dance and socialize. A playdate with dancing would be great."

Before she knew what was happening, the mothers were surrounding her, telling her all the reasons they would love for her to teach a dance class. The only dance studio within driving distance was not very welcoming and had asked several of the parents to not bring their children back.

Catalina knew all too well how it felt not to be wanted. "We can meet two or three times a week if they want to."

By the end of the party, she had six students in a class she never knew she'd wanted to teach, but it felt so right. Franny asked to take Willa home for the evening.

Holding the chest containing the tea set,

Catalina's mom frowned. "It's been a long day: I should take her home so she can get some rest."

Andres moved to his mother. It looked as if he was going to argue with Laura. Catalina stepped next to her mother. "I think that's a good idea. Mom, it will give you time to check in with Dad. After I clean up here, I'll pick her up and we can have a special dinner together."

With everyone gone, she took a minute for herself to sit and watch the water before finishing the cleanup. The day hadn't been as bad as she had feared. It had actually turned out pretty well.

She sighed, closed her eyes and sent up a prayer of thanks. Rolling her neck, she released the tension.

"So you're teaching dance again?" The deep voice tightened her skin. Andres slipped onto the bench next to her.

"I am. I didn't see that coming, but I'm excited."

"Are you sure it's a smart thing to start

up? Those kids will start counting on you. They won't understand when you leave or get bored."

That stung. "I never got bored of dancing."

"Be honest. You have a history of running when you get bored or things get too hard. Dance was just one of many things you didn't finish."

"It wasn't like that with dance." Or you. But she wasn't brave enough to share that secret part of her heart.

"Then why did you quit? You had plans to do bigger shows, but you dropped them all and just walked away."

"It wasn't my choice. I never left dance willingly." Her fingers twisted around each other. "Some of my grades weren't as good as they should have been. I was actually failing one class. My father thought I was wasting time and energy on dance. He said he wouldn't pay for my lessons or studio time until I had all As. I never could have made straight As. So, me being me, I decided to lash out."

She sighed. "I told him it didn't matter. I didn't want to dance anyway. I let my pride get in the way. I had started taking classes in college, but then I found out I was pregnant and…" She shrugged. "I had more important things to focus on. Like how I was going to support my baby. I never wanted to need money from my father again."

"I didn't know." He was quiet for a moment. "Well, you were really good with the kids. I just don't want them to get attached to you and then you leave. They won't understand. They'll be hurt when you walk away from them."

Her heart twisted at his unsaid words. She had walked away from him with their baby. The wound she left was so deep, would he ever truly be able to forgive her?

She resisted the urge to curl up and shut down. "I'm so sorry, Andres. Going forward I'll be very honest with them. Maybe I can find someone to help so there's a smooth transition. I never meant to hurt anyone."

Thinking of her counselor's words, she took a deep breath and looked to the endless horizon. She was a new person in Christ. "I'm not that girl anymore. When anxiety took over, it was better for me to cut and run. It was the only strategy I had at the time."

His profile was strong and rigid, then he nodded and turned to her. "I guess it means something that you are here now. The hurt is harder to let go of than I realized. Thank you for trying to make it right. Today was the first time I got a glimpse of the girl I used to know."

"You were the only one who knew her. You were the only one who came close to understanding me. Accepting me."

"It wasn't enough, though, was it? In the last six years, I've learned how important roots are to me. Port Del Mar and my family are my roots. Roots I want to give my daughter."

"I want to give her roots, too, but they don't have to be in Port Del Mar." They could be in Canada. Should she say something now? And when it didn't happen, he'd be upset for no reason. There was already so much emotional distance between them. The acid in her stomach turned and twisted.

She crossed her arms over her middle. "We can give her family roots anywhere. It's not about a place, but people. She doesn't have to be here to understand she has family who love her and support her."

He turned and gently touched her face, lifting her chin until they were face-to-face. "I let you run from me six years ago. I won't let you run with my daughter."

She fought back the urge to cry. "Six years ago, you didn't fight very hard to keep me." As soon as the words were out, she wanted to bring them back.

That was her secret to bury. Late at

night she would clutch the phone close to her and listen to his messages and silently plead with him to break through the barriers her father had put in place. She had prayed for Andres to be strong enough to fight her father so they could be together. She knew she was too weak. But that wasn't fair to him.

The truth wasn't that Andres didn't have the strength; it was that she wasn't worth the effort. The last thing he needed was a spoiled rich girl who didn't know the first thing about surviving on her own.

Now it wasn't her he wanted. It was Willa.

"I'm not running anymore. Any decision I make now is to build a better future for Willa and me."

"Willa's future includes me." His words were a hard line in the sand. No room for argument.

"Of course." She would not cry for the little girl inside her who was never good enough. No one wanted to keep her. Now the only value she had to anyone was that she was Willa's mother. "I knew you'd be a great father. Willa needs you in her life. We should focus on what we can do while we are here. Like Thanksgiving. My mother really wants to host it at her house so that my father can be there. Your whole family is invited. I know they don't want to eat at the big house, but that's Willa's home, too." Her heart pounded in her ears. His father might never agree to a family gathering with her parents. "We need to come together on this. Please."

"Thanksgiving at your house? I'll work on my parents. We'll be there. What about next Wednesday? I have the day off. She could spend Tuesday night with my parents. You can join us for dinner. I want to have more time with just her and me."

She'd known it was coming. "Okay."

This was it. He would be a part of Willa's life, and she had to let it happen. She wanted to be a better person. She wanted that little girl curled up in her heart to have enough self-confidence in her worth and value as a child of God that others' disapproval didn't crush her.

Willa's loving him and his family didn't take away from her. She had told her mother that very thing. Now it seemed she needed to remind herself. God had a plan. It would all work out, even if it wasn't what she wanted.

Chapter Seven

Willa had been darting between the floor-to-ceiling front windows for over an hour as Catalina, Trevor and her mother pushed through cooking the first Thanksgiving meal they had ever prepared themselves. The little girl finally saw what she had been waiting for.

"Here they come, GiGi!" She ran to the edge of the table that was set for twelve, bouncing in front of her grandmother. "They're here. GiGi, they're here."

"Willemina, inside voice. You need to act like a lady." Holding out her hand, GiGi waited for Willa to take it. "Let's leave your mother here to greet them and we'll get you a clean dress." Her gaze went over Willa's appearance. "And your hair needs to be fixed again."

Willa looked down at her dress, then to Catalina. "Mama, what's wrong with my dress? It's my favorite. I wanted to wear it for Daddy."

Catalina glared at her mother. "She's fine. Washing your hands is a good idea, though."

Her mother rolled her eyes. "There is nothing wrong with looking nice for guests."

Willa looked confused. "But I thought I did look nice. And this is Daddy and his family. They aren't guests."

The deep door chimes rang throughout the house. "Go wash your hands and check your hair. If you think it needs to be redone, your GiGi can help."

"Okay." With a huge grin, Willa grabbed Laura's hand and ran for the bathroom in the hallway.

With a deep breath, Catalina went to the door. Putting a smile on her face, she opened it.

"Happy Thanksgiving," she greeted the Sanchez family. There were varying looks of hesitation on all six faces. Catalina stepped back. "Come in. Come in."

Franny was the first to step forward. She gave Catalina a warm hug.

"I know your mother said not to bring anything, but we have a few family favorites that we wanted to share. Eva made my honey pecan yams." Stepping back, she gestured toward her daughter. "And it's not Thanksgiving without pumpkin empanadas and sopaipilla cheesecake."

Andres lifted the container holding the cheesecake. Maya held another dish.

Catalina's mouth watered. "Thank you. It's been too long since I've had these goodies. Everyone will love them."

She took the platter of pumpkin empanadas from Maya and went toward the dining room. "Follow me. We'll put everything in here. We decided to set it up as a self-serve buffet."

Willa rushed into the room, heading straight for her father, colliding with him as she wrapped him in a well-executed tackle. This time he was able to stay on his feet.

"Willemina Wimberly, that is not how you greet people." GiGi's voice was stern.

"But Daddy said I could tackle him whenever I wanted. And I'm so happy I have bubbles inside that want to explode."

Andres laughed. "Exploding bubbles?"

Catalina stood next to her mom and put her arm around her. "Everything's ready. We're just waiting for Trevor. He's bringing Dad in."

Her mother pulled out her shining hostess smile, the one she always used when inviting movers and shakers of Texas into their ranch home. This year was different. Everything was different.

"There will be one empty place at the table. Krystal couldn't make it. She had to be out of the country, and there was just no way to get back in time." She smiled. "Oh, look. Noah brought his guitar. You'll play for us after dinner?"

"Yes, ma'am." He shifted his weight and lifted his gaze to the winding staircase and landing above them.

Franny patted his shoulder. "Willa said she wanted us to sing. If I remember correctly, Cat had such a beautiful voice."

Maya was at her other side. "She was always willing to join us. She has the sweetest voice."

"She does? I don't remember her singing. She did like making loud noises." Laura Wimberly had never encouraged Catalina in any of the arts. "She had a bad habit of screaming her favorite songs to annoy her father and me."

Franny cleared her throat and moved close to Catalina, taking her hand in hers. "She did love to sing. My kitchen was full of voices. One more just made it sweeter."

Catalina wanted to hug Franny. Her

mother hadn't meant to insult her, she understood that now, but at ten her mother's stern criticism of her singing had been crushing. The house had been so big and quiet. The way her parents liked it. "Back then, I worked very hard to annoy them. So they might not have heard the best use of my voice."

Franny gave her a sweet, understanding smile, then moved to her husband and took his hand. Catalina had loved to sing, and it gave her joy. Joy she wanted to give her daughter.

"How are the dance lessons going?" Franny asked, filling the now-awkward silence. "Did you find a place?"

"Yes. I had a few more kids join us." She turned to Andres. "Remind me to give you the schedule we worked up with the parents. You can stop by if you want. It's so much fun. The kids are having a great time."

"Yes, I went to one of the practices and they were lovely." Mrs. Wimberly stopped in front of Willa and smoothed a strand of rebellious curls back into place. "God had it already worked out. Just like today. It's not what any of us expected, but it's good."

Her mother looked at Franny, her smile actually the warmest Catalina had ever seen it. "If we trust God, the best things happen the way they should, without our interference. That's a lesson I've been learning lately."

"Yes. God's plans are always much better than ours, if we can only trust. That's something I think we all struggle with." Catalina could see the tension leave Franny as she agreed with her mother.

Trevor came in from the opposite direction, walking slowly with their dad. The ever-present oxygen machine followed them. Tubing was attached like a leash. This was the first time Catalina had seen her father walking in two weeks.

It was good, but it still took her aback a little bit to see how her father had aged in the last month. He was not the larger-than-life robust man who had always filled the room with his presence.

"I'm going to check on the last few items. Catalina," her mother said in a hushed voice. "Please, take our guests into the dining room."

Catalina herded everyone into the formal dining room and helped Franny arrange the new dishes on the buffet lining the wall. The dark oak cabinet on the other side held the apple and pecan pies they had purchased in town. They added the Sanchez treats.

Her mother had reduced the size of the dining table, and it was set for twelve. The crystal stemware sparkled, and china gleamed. Gold-painted pumpkins and fall foliage ran along the center of the table.

Handwritten name tags had been placed around the table, so everyone mingled looking for theirs.

"I found my name." Willa jumped up and down. She was wearing the same dress she'd been wearing earlier, along with her favorite purple cowboy boots. "Look, Daddy! You're next to me, and Mama, you're on my other side."

Catalina was a little surprised that her mother had placed them together as a family.

She invited everyone to sit down as they chatted about the weather and the ranch. Her mother had put José next to her father at one end of the table. Trevor helped Mr. Wimberly settle in, then took his seat on his other side. It was still strange to witness the unexpected role of caretaker her brother had willing stepped into. But their father's illness had changed everything.

For the first time, Catalina was seated next to her mother. The empty chair was on the other side. Across from Cat. Her mother was always very strategic with placing people in an order that would benefit her agenda. She spent a moment trying to figure everything out, but then decided it wasn't worth it.

This was a memory in the making. One she never thought would happen. All of her favorite people were at the same table. Her two families were one for this slip of time. She wanted every moment to be imprinted in her brain.

No, no. Tears burned the back of her eyes. She couldn't cry. They wouldn't understand that her heart was just overflowing with thankfulness and gratitude. How many times she'd imagined the Sanchez family eating dinner with her family. She glanced over Willa's head and studied Andres. He was leaning forward, listening to her father. They were talking ranch business with José and Trevor.

Her mother stood to get everyone's attention. "Thank you for being here. Today is a special day set aside so that we remember to stop and give thanks for all that the Lord is giving us. It's easy to lose sight of our blessings in the stress of what we think is important. I would love for everyone to give thanks for one thing. I know there is more, but for now just add one to our prayer of Thanksgiving. I'll start."

She reached out her hands and waited for everyone to join her. They all stood. "Thank you, God, for bringing our precious granddaughter, Willa, to our family. She's brought us so much joy."

The next person was Noah, and the prayers moved around to the table as each of the Sanchezes gave thanks for family, including Willa. Her daughter giggled next to her, feeling the outpouring of love.

It came to Andres and Catalina assumed he would echo the others. After a pause, he sighed. "I need to give thanks for Catalina. I..."

Her heart tightened as they waited for him to finish. She hadn't done anything to deserve his gratitude.

He cleared his throat. "I think it's in Deuteronomy. Be strong. Have courage. Don't fear. I'm so thankful for her courage when I know she must have been so afraid. Thank you, Cat."

She kept her head down and bit her lip so the tears wouldn't fall. Andres bumped their daughter. "Your turn, *mijita*."

"I give thanks for this big table at GiGi's house. It's so big it can hold all my family. I'm thankful for my new horse so I can be a cowboy like Buelito and PawPaw. I pray that we can live on the ranch forever. I'm thankful for the frogs that sing at night. I hope one day Mama and Daddy will live in the same house and we can be family like we are right now."

That train of thought had to be stopped. "One, Willa."

"Oh yes." She squeezed Cat's hand and looked up at her with a grin. "Your turn, Mama."

Her throat was still raw from holding back her emotions. "I'm so thankful for all the family support."

Eva was the last to go. She kept it short, and soon they were all sitting, passing the dishes of food around. Jose said that he'd have the ranch hands pull the Christmas decorations out of the barn and decorate the gate tomorrow.

Willa got to her knees to set down her glass of milk. "How do you get to the top? The Wimberly sign is very tall."

"We use a cherry picker to wrap the garland and lights. The red and silver ornaments are bigger than your head." Jose grinned at his granddaughter.

"I want to help! That sounds like fun. What's a cherry picker?" Willa asked, her face shining with excitement.

"It's like a crane with a bucket. So, we can reach the top of tall things." Her buelito explained.

"Will you be decorating tomorrow, too, Mrs. Wimberly?" Franny asked as she cut her turkey.

Catalina didn't miss the brief shadow of sadness that floated across her mother's face. She turned to the large window that looked out over the front of the ranch.

From here, the front gate was very small, but you could make out the ironwork that spelled out *Wimberly Cattle Company* arching over the entryway. "I usually have a company out of Houston come and decorate the house."

"Mom." Trevor's one word sounded exasperated.

Laura Wimberly sat a little straighter and shot a glare at her son. It was so fast and subtle most people probably wouldn't notice, but Catalina knew that Trevor had canceled the design firm.

Her mother smiled, then shook her head. "I'm not sure what I'll do this year. We won't be hosting the usual parties. I don't think we will be decorating this year. But I am excited about taking Willa to the Christmas by the Sea festivities in town."

"GiGi." Willa practically stood in her chair. "It's Christmas, and you have these big windows that are perfect for big trees. I want to go to Christmas by the Sea and I can help decorate."

"She's right, Mom." It hadn't even occurred to Catalina that her mother wouldn't be decorating for Christmas. "It's Willa's first Christmas here at the ranch. Decorating can be a family affair. We don't have to go all fancy. Growing up, I loved helping Franny and her kids. We had so much fun. Let's do it here."

"Willa should have a tree." Her father's voice had the commanding tone that no one argued with from the days before his illness.

"But Calvin, there are six trees. Maybe more. There's so much. It took a team of eight workers to get it all set up in a day."

"Mom, all we need is one tree for the front living room in the bay window."

"It's not just the tree. With all the different themes, I'm sure we have almost a hundred boxes of decorations stored in the attic. It's such a hassle." Her mother sounded tired.

"With my boys here, we could have them down in no time. And I'm sure

Trevor would help, too. An extra empanada for everyone who helps." Franny placed her napkin over her plate. "They can pull them down and we can help set it up."

Catalina glanced at Andres. Was he upset that his mother had volunteered him?

"It's no problem. Sounds fun, right, *mijita*?" Andres offered.

Willa clapped her hands. "Yeah. Can we play Christmas music and make gingerbread men?"

Noah smiled brightly. "Decorating for Christmas is one of my favorite things if it gives me an extra pumpkin empanada."

Maya rolled her eyes. "You know as well as I do that Mom would give you an extra one anyway. Baby of the family gets what he wants." A teasing grin matched the gleam in her eye. "But if that makes you feel better, we can say that you get extras for helping. I can take down the boxes, too. I'm more helpful than Noah, anyway. He'll just start playing his guitar, claiming to be entertaining us."

"What's up with you saying the boys can carry the boxes down? I can do twice the amount of work as them with half the effort." Maya pointed to her head. "I know how to work smarter."

"Children." Franny looked down the table. "Yes. I called you *children* because that is how you are acting. Does this mean everyone is finished?" She looked at Laura at the opposite end of the table. "Please excuse their rudeness. I can help you clear off the table while the kids pull down your Christmas boxes. Not decorating this beautiful home would be a shame. We're all here. So, let us help."

"Mom, I know you were disappointed that we didn't hire Magnolia's Sweet Designs this year, but there was no need. We could do it now, as a family." Trevor put a hand on his dad's shoulder. "Hey, Dad, you want to get settled in your study so we can turn on the football game? It shouldn't take long to get a few boxes, and the games are about to start."

"I can watch the game in the living room where you'll be decorating. I want to see this."

As far as Catalina knew, her father had never taken an interest in the pre-Christmas activities. She really didn't remember him being here. Business usually had him traveling.

Laura blinked several times. Catalina wished that she was closer so she could reach for her mom's hand. Her mom was so stern that it was easy to forget how hard this year had been on her, too.

There was a part of her that was afraid her mother would turn down the offer of help because of pride. Catalina crossed her fork and knife on the top of her plate. "Franny, that's a great idea. Willa loves decorating."

She stood and started gathering dishes. "Franny and I can take everything to the kitchen. Mom, you know where all the

Christmas decorations are stored, right? You can take the team up there. With everyone here it shouldn't be too big a job."

There was a lot of attic space in the house. She and Trevor had never helped with the Christmas decorations before, so she wouldn't even know where to begin to look for them.

"Yay! Merry Christmas!" Willa cheered. "Do you have a star for the top of the tree? Can I put it on? We get to do this all together!" She hugged her arms tight to her chest and vibrated with excitement.

Laura stood and nodded. "I can't say no to that. Thank you so much for the offer. If you can take the dishes into the kitchen, I'll show them where the Christmas decorations are located. Then I'll come back and help put away the food."

Willa jumped up. "I want to see the attic. I can help. I'm fast and my muscles are really strong. Daddy, I can go with you." She wrapped herself around Andres's leg. "Please, let me help."

"Willa." She was not used to Willa asking someone else permission to do stuff.

"Daddy. I want to go with you." Willa pouted, turning her back to Catalina.

She sighed. Was Willa going to start playing them against each other? "I'm not sure it's safe."

Andres looked down at Willa, then to her. "Do you want her to come with us or help you with the dishes?"

He was asking her. Her idiotic heart skipped a beat then pooled, leaving her stomach warm. How was she going to co-parent with him if she turned gooey whenever he did something nice?

Breaking eye contact with him, she focused on Willa. "They have to go up into the attic. Uncle Trevor and GiGi will be helping them. That leaves PawPaw alone. How about I cut the sopaipilla cheesecake your Buelita made and you can take it to PawPaw? He'd like to spend time with you."

Her little lips twisted to the side as if

in deep thought. "Okay. I'll help PawPaw and eat cheesecake. But I'll get to help decorate, won't I?"

"We won't start without you."

Going to the kitchen with Franny, she worked in silence for the most part. The huge granite-and-stainless-steel kitchen was so different from the cozy, outdated space where Franny fed and loved her family.

Laura joined them as they dried the last gold-rimmed glass water goblet. She carried the platter with the leftover turkey and ham. "So much food. I don't want it to go to waste. Do you want to take it home, Franny? You have those four kids to feed."

"We're good." Andres's mother was a little stiff now that Laura had joined them in the kitchen. "But I could make some plates and take them to a few of the shut-ins we have around town. That's what we usually do."

"Oh, what a wonderful idea. I'm sure we have plenty of containers."

"All I need is a sturdy paper plate and foil."

Following her GiGi into the kitchen, Willa popped up on a stool at the counter. "What about gingerbread cookies? Buelita said when we decorated her house, we'd have some shaped like piggies with Mexican hot chocolate."

"You can't fill a house with Christmas love without them." Franny touched the tip of Willa's nose. "We'll have them at our house, tomorrow."

"But what about here? We need Christmas love here, too."

"Let's do it now." Laura went to her walk-in pantry, the one that was bigger than Franny's kitchen. She yelled back at them from deep inside. "I don't remember the last time I made cookies. Maybe with my grandmother. I'm sure we have all the ingredients. Franny, can you help me gather them and any utensils we'll need?"

Franny went into the pantry. A few moments later, both women came out, their arms full of bowls and all the supplies to make Christmas cookies.

Willa clapped. "I get to make cookies with both of my grandmothers! This is going to be the most outstanding Christmas!"

Her mother went to the kitchen laptop and soon had Christmas music playing throughout the house. For the first time in Catalina's memories, the house was full of true joy. The sound of laughter and the aroma of gingerbread filled the rooms and her heart.

How long could it last?

When they had flour on their faces and the counters covered in a chaotic cookie mess, Andres entered the kitchen, a frown on his face.

Was the baby spark of her new Christmas joy about to be put out?

Chapter Eight

Andres stopped under the archway leading into the Wimberly kitchen. It was like stepping into a fancy magazine spread and realizing he was wearing the wrong clothes. This was why he had stayed away from the big house. He didn't belong. But his daughter did, and he would stay for her.

His mother wiped her hands on a dish towel. "*Mijo*. What's wrong?" Concern etched her face.

"When she said she had almost a hundred boxes, she was not exaggerating. We were going to put up one tree but found

six. Eva and Noah challenged each other
to a tree-building contest, so now we
have two huge trees and so many boxes
we don't know where to start. We did go
with the white lights. We all decided that
was safe. But the boxes of decorations.
There's so many."

"Oh, *mijo*. You look shell-shocked." His
mother patted his face. "You scared me.
It can't be that bad."

"I thought you were just going to clean
the dishes? We have cookies now?"

Her mother shrugged. "Willa wanted
ginger cookies with hot chocolate when
we finished the tree. So we had to make
them now for later."

Andres was sure that made sense, but
today his brain was having processing issues. He had just had Thanksgiving at the
Wimberly table. And now he was decorating their house. When would he be allowed to go back to his normal world with
his daughter? In his mother's home, she
had four boxes for Christmas. *Four*. One

for the tree ornaments, one for wreaths and garland, another for the stockings and mantel decorations and the last one for the nativity sets. Four. That was normal.

The Wimberlys had countless boxes. It was like a giant Christmas store had exploded. His siblings were having a great time, but how did he compete with this?

"Uhm." He waved his hand to the room behind him. "We don't know what to do."

"The cookies need to chill," his mother told him, then turned to Laura. "What do you want done with the boxes?"

"Let's go and unpack those boxes. It's years of decorations. They weren't meant to be used all together. There are themes and I like to rotate them."

After putting the cookies in the industrial refrigerator, they straightened the counter and stacked the bowls.

In the living room, Catalina's father was laughing at Andres's sisters as they made a fashion show from the variety of

Christmas paraphernalia. Noah was playing his guitar.

When Andres entered the room with the moms, his sisters froze. They wore tree skirts, garland and gold curly things layered into crazy Christmas outfits.

Maya was the first to move. "So sorry. We were waiting and…well… We weren't sure what you wanted done next."

A bomb of Christmas colors had gone off in the middle of the huge living space. Andres couldn't bring himself to call it a room. It was too vast. It was like three rooms without walls.

Large tubs of many colors filled the space by the bay window. It could have been a room all by itself. There was now a disarray of decorations from rustic ranch to frilly Victorian, the various years and themes all clashing.

He couldn't read Mrs. Wimberly's expression. Was she mad? Overwhelmed?

"Oh, these are so pretty." Maya and Eva pulled colored glass ornaments from a box that was much older than either of them. "They look so old. Are they replicas?"

"No." Laura joined his sisters. "These belonged to my mother-in-law. They were the only thing allowed on the tree as long as I knew her. She refused to let me change them or add anything to it. She said they were Wimberly heirlooms and should be the only thing used to decorate. Tradition was everything to her. She didn't really like me, said I was too modern all the time."

"Really?" Catalina sounded as surprised as he felt.

Trevor laughed. "They would get after it. Once, Mom got so mad she said she wasn't going to bring us back to the ranch unless Gran apologized to her. That was before you were born. By the time you came along, we had lost Gran, and Mom could do what she wanted."

Mr. Wimberly coughed. "My mother had a certain notion of how things should go. She didn't like it if someone—" with one brow raised, he cut a subtle glance at his wife "—dared to disagree. She didn't like being told otherwise."

Slapping the arm of his chair, he gave a low laugh. "Careful, Trevor. Wimberly men must like that bullheaded trait in women. Maybe you've been wise to stay away from relationships."

"Calvin Lawrence Wimberly."

"Hey, look at this," Trevor yelled. It was obvious to everyone in the room that he wanted to change the subject fast. He had a large plastic bin on the leather sofa. "It's Cat dancing as a reindeer." He flipped the Popsicle-stick frame. "She's in the fourth grade. She was always dancing around."

"She was a dancer." Franny sat down at the other side of the box.

Willa gasped. "Pictures of Mama dancing?" Taking Cat's hand, she pulled her over to the sofa.

Cat's mom took the framed picture from Trevor. "She was a beautiful dancer."

Willa cuddled up next to his mother

and lifted a red string with a handprint painted like a reindeer with googly eyes and glitter. "I love this." She looked up at her buelita. "I can't read cursive."

Franny carefully tilted it to read the writing. "It says, 'Merry Christmas, love, Cat. Second grade.'" Willa pulled another one out, a misshapen snowflake covered in silver glitter with a picture of a very young Catalina. "Mama! It's you."

"These are all Christmas ornaments made by Catalina." Franny frowned.

"No." Laura's expression had tightened. "Hers are just on top. She's twelve years younger than Trevor, fourteen younger than Krystal. By the time she was making hers, they had stopped. They're stacked in order."

Everyone gathered around the box. Each ornament had been carefully stored in layers of tissue paper. As they pulled each thin layer out, they found Trevor's and Krystal's. Ornaments documenting their childhood were soon spread across the floor. At the bottom was a manger formed of Popsicle sticks that Krystal had made in preschool.

"Mom, I don't remember ever seeing these before." Cat sounded confused.

With a heavy sigh, her mother placed an angel Trevor had made back in the box. "They didn't fit the themes. I didn't know what to do with them, so each year I wrapped them in tissue paper and added them to the box."

Andres couldn't believe that every gift the Wimberly kids made for their parents was put away, never to be seen again. The Sanchez tree was full of awkward, poorly designed kids' crafts. Eva had gone through a purple stage, and each year the ornaments were pulled out and it was remembered. He knelt beside Cat and picked up a star containing a third-grade picture of Trevor. "How about we use them all to decorate the tree this year?"

"Can we, Mom?" Willa held up a paper

gingerbread house with a stern five-year-old Krystal in the tiny window.

Cat took in all the mismatched and far-from-perfect child-made ornaments. They hadn't been good enough for the Wimberly tree. "I don't know. Your GiGi has a theme each year. Maybe some of them can be worked in." She looked for the best ones. "Mom, what do you want for this year's tree?"

There was no answer, so she looked up. Her mother was sitting on the floor with her legs tucked under her, holding a twisted heart made of clay. Maybe they were supposed to be candy canes?

Catalina grinned. Even she had to admit that that one was a bit on the hideous side. "Trevor must have made that one. He was never good at putting colors together."

"Hey. Red and green are Christmas colors. I didn't know they turned brown when you mixed them."

"Look at this one." Andres lifted a wreath made from green cutouts of Catalina's preschool hands. They weren't all going in the same direction, so it looked a little haphazard.

She remembered working so hard, knowing this would be the one her parents loved. "It's a wreath, but it looks more like a cactus with the fingers poking every which way."

Willa took it. "The hands are so small. Who made this one?"

"Your mom. You can tell because they're all going different directions." Andres grinned.

"I was being creative." She laughed. "Mom?" Her mother's head was still down. "Can we use a few of these?"

Laura looked up. Catalina was surprised to see the moisture in her mother's eyes. "Mom?"

"I hid these away because…" Laura glanced at Willa. "Well, I didn't think they would fit in with the…the other decorations." Her voice was low.

"But they're so pretty," Willa said, not understanding.

"Yes, they are." Laura reached across and tweaked Willa's nose. "This year's theme is memories. We'll use the big red satin ribbon and the gold silk with little metal stars as the garland. There are gold curly bunches and all the handmade ornaments."

"There's a box full of beautiful angels. Can we use them, too?" Eva asked.

With a nod, Laura agreed. "We need Willa to make an ornament to add to the tree. I have paper in my office. What do you want to make with your handprints?"

Eva and Maya wrapped the garlands around the trees and everyone else hung the ornaments. Laura gave them a lesson about size and placement before she left to find the supplies for Willa to make her own ornament.

Willa ran from box to box, then to the tree. "This one is red, white and gold! It's my favorite. Or the silver one with glitter. I like glitter!"

Andres's father said that the animals

didn't take the day off and that he was going to check the feeders. Franny went to the kitchen to finish the cookies, and Trevor quietly took their father back to his study.

Andres's sisters and brother didn't seem to have any problem hanging out in the Wimberly house. They were teasing Catalina just like they had done when she came to their home. Willa was giggling at something Noah was telling her.

Maya elbowed Andres. "You're going to scare the reindeer away with that scowl. What's going on? You're spending the day with your daughter. You should be happy. Smile."

"I am happy." He heard the grumble in his voice.

She laughed out loud, causing everyone to turn and look at them.

"We're just about finished." Eva pulled out her phone. "We need a few pictures for our first Christmas decorating party with Willa. She can put the tree topper on this one."

Willa dug through a few boxes until she found a beautiful vintage glass silver topper from her great-grandmother's collection. "Mama. What about this one?"

Cat bent over to inspect the work of art, and Andres's breath caught at the sight of mother and daughter. His sister was right. He had every reason to be happy. Being angry wasn't going to help him build a relationship with his daughter.

Anger was a protective device to keep Cat at arm's length, but he couldn't hold on to it without permanent damage to his heart. His daughter was now his heart. This was not going to be easy.

"Daddy, can you help me put the star on top of the tree?"

Cat's eyes went wide. "I thought I'd…"

"Let your mom help—"

"But you're taller."

"Why don't you both help her?" Eva suggested. "That would be a great picture." She waved them to the tallest tree. "Put her on your shoulders, and Cat, put your hand on her leg."

Willa giggled. "I'm so tall. Mama, I'm taller than you."

Mother and daughter. They would be in his life forever now. Cat was so close. Could she hear his heartbeat?

How had her parents not seen her for the gift she was? She had been put in a box and told to stay out of sight, just like the ornaments that hadn't been good enough for the trees.

He lifted Willa higher so she could reach the top. Her little tongue poked out as she concentrated on her job. Cat climbed halfway up the ladder on the other side of the tree. From there, she helped Willa secure the glass star. Willa clapped.

"Nice job, ladies." His hand tightened around his daughter's little waist. She was so small. Catalina beamed at him. The Cat he had fallen in love with years ago.

Not the spoiled rich girl, but the lonely girl who just wanted to belong.

Willa giggled as she placed her hand in his hair to help her balance. "It's so pretty. I want to stay up here all night."

"Oh, but the best place to see the tree is lying under it with all the lights above you. With hot chocolate and gingerbread in your tummy." Cat reached up and tickled her. Her warmth mingled with Willa's and he was wrapped in the middle of their love.

This moment was how he had always imagined the holidays would be when he had his own family, but it was also all wrong. Catalina didn't belong to him. She was a Wimberly and they were at the Wimberly house.

A flash went off. He had forgotten his sister was taking pictures.

Laura stood in the wide doorway. "You are a little decorator. It's beautiful. I think it's my favorite tree to date. It will be even better once you have your ornament on it." She held up a caddy full of sparkly art supplies. "We can work in the kitchen and check on the cookies."

"Daddy, put me down!" Willa wiggled right out of his arms as she ran to her GiGi.

"You lost her to arts and crafts. Don't worry, she'll be back." Cat bumped his shoulder.

He snorted. "For claiming she wanted to be on my shoulders all night, it didn't take her long to scramble down and run to her GiGi." His arms already felt empty.

"These are great pictures. I'm going to show Mom." Maya waved her phone at them.

"And eat the first batch of cookies right out of the oven." Noah headed straight for the kitchen. "No, you don't."

"Hey, I want fresh cookies, too." Eva ran after them, sounding more like a ten-year-old than a twenty-one-year-old.

Cat chuckled. "I love being around your

sisters and brother. I wish I had that kind of relationship with mine."

"The kind where they leave you to clean up the mess?" He waved around the room, then looked up at her. That last-pup-in-the-shelter look always got to him. "Hey. They're so much older than you. Y'all didn't have a chance to build one. They were off to school and internships by the time you were eight." He remembered a little girl so lonely she had practically moved in with them during the summers. No one from the big house had even seemed to notice.

She picked up random decorations from the heaps scattered across the vast room and packed them away. "Yeah. I know. It was one of the reasons I loved being at your house so much. For all intents and purposes, I was an only child. I always wanted to be a part of a big boisterous family. When I was younger, I thought maybe I'd been left at the front door and they took me in out of pity." She laughed as she secured a lid on one of the boxes.

Every movement was quick but elegant. She never could sit still for long. Her body and mind were in perpetual motion. He gathered up the garland draped haphazardly over the sofa and stuffed it in a box. "There're enough decorations here to cover the whole town."

"You say that as if it's a bad thing." She laughed and threw a large blue ball covered in pheasant feathers at him.

Easily catching it, he held it up and studied it. "What is this? What does it have to do with Christmas?" He tossed it in a box of assorted ornaments. It was probably the wrong box. Good. "You don't think this is all a waste? It was used once or twice, then forgotten."

He sighed. His sister was right. The bad mood didn't belong on a day of thanksgiving, but he couldn't shake it.

This was not how he was supposed to

enter fatherhood. Catalina approached him and put a hand over his heart.

"I'm so sorry. I know this isn't how you pictured your first holiday as a father. You've made it very clear how you feel about my family. But they are as much in Willa's makeup as your family is. I can't change that."

Great. Now she was reading his mind. "Maybe you were onto something and you were adopted."

With a smirk, she slapped his upper arm and stepped back. "They'd still be my family."

"True."

"I'm really sorry. I don't know what else to do to make this up to you. My father was horrid, and I didn't fight him as much as I should have. I didn't trust God enough to do the right thing. But I'm here now. Today was a good beginning for our families. Don't you think?"

There was pain in her eyes that hadn't

been there earlier today. It was his fault. He'd passed his bad mood on to her.

"What I said at dinner was true." She was too far away from him.

He took a step closer to her and lifted her chin so that they were eye to eye. "I admire your courage. I know the strength it took to stand against your father. You protected our daughter the best you could. She's magnificent. Just in the short time I've known her, I can't imagine my life without her. It might not be the way I pictured fatherhood. But she's my daughter. Thank you."

Her lips parted as if she was going to say something, but she didn't. He waited.

Her eyes searched his. The blood pounded in his ears. He wasn't sure if she leaned into him or he moved to her, but somehow their lips made contact.

For a second, all the confusion of the world vanished and everything was right. For years now, he had buried the reasons he had fallen in love with her under anger and hurt.

Her fingers reached for his hands.

Everything good and sweet was in her kiss. He took more, deepening the touch. It was like finding a tall, cool glass of water when you didn't even know you were thirsty. He wanted to guzzle. To take his fill after a long drought. Then he was alone.

Blinking at the abrupt change, Andres stared at her. Her hand was over her mouth, her eyes wide.

"I can't believe we did that." She shook her head, then looked over her shoulder. "If Willa had seen that, she'd be so confused. Or hopeful that we were getting together."

He was confused. He opened his mouth to say something, then realized he didn't know what to say. Like a fish flung onto a boat deck, he gasped and floundered. How had this even happened?

They needed to get back on track and

focused. Picking up the scattered angels, he tossed around a way to bring up a topic that he knew would cause a fight. Custody of Willa.

Should he wait? Today had gone better than he had imagined it would. Of course, he had pictured a worst-case scenario, and the Wimberlys had been much more gracious than he had given them credit for. Maybe he was as much the problem as they were.

That didn't sit well with him. On one of the leather chairs was an antler with holly tied to it. It looked more like a weapon than a Christmas ornament. He shook his head. Money just couldn't buy good taste.

He snorted. Not like he had the right to be pointing fingers. That kiss proved his own lack of clear thinking. But the anger and hurt were more of a faded photo than vibrant red paint splattered across his heart and mind.

Ceramic carolers smiled at him. They didn't even know they were lost. No Dickensian village in sight. He riffled through some of the boxes. So much greenery but no little town.

Taking a deep breath, he finally made himself look for Cat. She was at the stone fireplace. It was almost big enough for her to walk into. Reaching up to the rough wood mantel, she held little houses and a church in her hands.

"I think these guys belong in your Christmas town." He went over and helped set up the rest of the village on a fluffy white sheet. "Obviously not in Texas."

She laughed. "Canada, perhaps? Have you ever been that far north?"

"Nope. It looks nice, though. I have a friend who's up there for a few months a year. He's always showing me pictures." He placed the trio of singers under a lamppost. "Now they're happy at home." This was his opening. "It's good to have a home you can count on with people you love."

She stopped what she was doing but

didn't look at him. "It is. Making a home for me and Willa is a dream of mine."

"Today's been great. Better than I thought it would go. I've been thinking." He paused. He had to get this right. "You said your job is flexible and you can do it from anywhere and anytime as long as you get your projects done. If you lived in Port Del Mar, I could take Willa to school in the mornings or pick her up, depending on my shifts. Going to the school and eating lunch with her would be easy. I'd be a part of her everyday life." His mouth went dry. "It makes sense, right?" Why did it feel like the first time he'd asked a girl to the school dance? Pressure pushed on his chest.

Catalina took a step back and crossed her arms over her middle. The blackened fireplace became something of great interest. She was doing everything possible to avoid his gaze.

His stomach dropped, and he swallowed back the taste of fear. He didn't have to be an expert in body language to pick up her hints.

He rushed ahead before she could build an argument against his idea. "You don't have to stay here in the big house. I know you don't want to live with your parents. They have cottages and houses all over the property. You could be independent."

Her jaw bounced as she clenched and unclenched the muscle. After a long minute of silence, she shook her head.

"At least consider it. Please." He wasn't above begging or pleading. "If you take her back to Austin, I'll be reduced to an every-other-weekend dad. That's not the kind of father I want to be. I thought of moving to Austin, but the sheriff's department needs me. I have an obligation here. There are people that count on me."

She was stone-faced.

He ran his hand through his hair. "Is it me? You don't want to deal with me on a daily basis. I'm sorry about the kiss. We can set rules. Our parents can be the go-between. No direct communication unless you want it." He was sounding desperate, but he didn't care. He couldn't imagine his life without Willa in it every day.

There was no way for him to be a full-time dad. if she lived six hours away. "I could move to Austin, but your job sounds flexible. I can't..." He closed his mouth. He took a deep breath. "Would you even consider moving to Port Del Mar?"

She lifted her gaze until they were eye to eye, then she shook her head.

"Stop shaking your head. Talk to me. Explain why you have to live in Austin."

"It's not about me living in Austin. I have a plan to be fully independent of my parents. The company I work for has an unexpected opening in upper management. It's a great opportunity. I would be the creative director of some pretty big projects. My income would almost double. The benefits are great. If I'm careful, in five years I'd be right where I want financially. I haven't been offered the job yet.

There were three of us for the last round of interviews."

She pressed her lips together and looked to the top of the Christmas tree. The vintage star winked at them. Then she looked down.

"Cat." This was bad. He cleared his throat. "That does sound like a great opportunity. So, would you have to stay in Austin if you were offered the job?"

"No. Not Austin. I'm there because that's where I finished college. I've been to the headquarters three times. Twice as an intern, then in the first round of the interviews. Everything else has been online." Her shoulders went back, as if she was gathering her courage.

"Where are the headquarters?" Dread made his vision swim a bit.

"Toronto."

He blinked. "The only Toronto I know is in Canada."

"If I took the job, I would need to be there. As creative director, I'd need to work at the headquarters more often. I still have some flexibility and it's a great vacation plan. I've already mapped out a schedule to bring Willa to Texas at least once a quarter. You could come up for long weekends. We could work it out so that she spends time with you every month. I haven't gotten the offer. So it might not even matter."

"You're doing it again." He turned away. He was such an idiot for believing her. "When were you going to tell me?"

Turning back to her, he pointed a finger. "You introduce me to my daughter and then you make plans to take her to Canada. Canada, really? That is not a day-trip in the car. I thought six hours to Austin was too far. Now you want to…" He clamped his mouth shut and stomped to the other side of the room. He needed to think this through and not say anything he'd regret. Deep, calming breaths didn't help collect his sorry self.

A clear brain and rational thought were

what he needed, but the only word that was racing around was *Canada*. She was taking his daughter to Canada.

Chapter Nine

Catalina swallowed hard. Guilt, pain and fear tasted pretty nasty. "Andres, I know it sounds so far away. But my plans are to be up there for only a few years. Five at the most."

He spun back around to her. "Five years? I've already lost the first five. She'll be ten before you make it back to Texas. Would you even come back to Port Del Mar? Maybe Paris next? You're running away again. These last few weeks, I thought maybe you had changed, but I feel like I've been sucker-punched all over again. Why did I think it would be any different this time?"

"Because it is different. I'm different." She had to stay calm and talk through this. "I'm not running away from you. I'm running to an opportunity." She waved her arms to what he assumed she thought was north. "I'm not taking this lightly. I've spent as many hours working on a plan to keep you and Willa in touch as I have researching the job. Willa comes first, but I can still pursue my dreams. I want to be a role model for my daughter. I promise between me coming to Texas and you visiting, you'll be able to see Willa at least once a month."

"Ha. That's great." His jaw tightened as he turned from her. His breathing came harder as he pushed his fist against the frame around the window. "I've missed the first five years and now for the next five I get to see her briefly every four to five weeks." Pushing away from the window he looked straight at her, eyes burning. "No, thank you."

She'd never seen him this close to violence. "We both have careers that we care about. This can work, if we keep an open mind and communicate."

"You only told me because I asked you to leave Austin. When was I going to find out?"

"I didn't see any reason to tell you until I knew there was even a chance. I would talk to you before I made my final decision."

His sarcastic laugh burned her ears.

"How terribly considerate of you. I think it's time we got some legal paperwork drawn up."

"No. I don't want lawyers involved with our relationship with Willa."

"And I don't want my daughter to be taken off to Canada."

Arms crossed, they mirrored each other. Neither said a word as they stared the other down. The last time they had stood like this, she had wanted to ride a new stallion that had just been brought in from Oklahoma. Her father had said no, and Andres had agreed with him.

Yes, at times he and her father had been on the same side. Against her. And she had hated it. He had claimed to be protecting her from herself. "You always thought you knew what was best for me."

"You had some strong self-destructive behaviors. Is this one of them? Or is going to Canada easier than staying and dealing with me?"

"No. It's a great opportunity, but not an easy choice. It hasn't been easy at all."

They went back to being silent.

"Are we interrupting something?" Noah hovered in the archway.

His sister bumped into him. "Ay! Why did you stop in the middle of the hallway?"

"*Pelea de amantes*," Noah answered in a stage whisper.

"Who's fighting?" Willa pushed her way between them as she entered the room.

"This is not a lovers' quarrel," Andres answered between clenched teeth, glaring at his brother. "No one is fighting."

He popped his neck, then turned to their daughter with a smile on his face.

She ran to him and leaped at him with full confidence that he would catch her. "Look, Daddy. I made two." She lifted the ornaments to show him. "This one is my hand. GiGi traced it and I added the glitter."

"That's pretty. Is that the picture from today?" He took the other one. She had made a Christmas tree from twigs and in the middle was the picture of the three of them placing the topper on the tree.

"When Eva showed it to me, I sent it straight to my printer." Laura sounded as excited as everyone else. "Her first Christmas with both of her parents."

"GiGi and Buelita, Tía Eva, Tía Maya and Tío Noah made ornaments, too." After handing her art to Andres, Willa ran to her grandmothers and grabbed their hands.

They each put their ornaments on the

tree. Noah picked up his guitar and softly played some classic Christmas songs.

"Mama, Aunt Krystal and Uncle Trevor already have ones here." She danced around the tree, touching all the ones they'd hung up earlier. "Now we can all have an ornament on the family tree." And then she gasped and covered her mouth. "What about PawPaw and Buelito?"

Catalina knelt in front of her daughter. "PawPaw is really tired now. How about we make one with him tomorrow? Just the three of us?"

Willa nodded, then looked at her dad. "Can Daddy and Buelito join us? They need to make theirs." She took Andres's hand. "You have to come back tomorrow, Daddy."

"We can make it with your Buelito at their house."

"GiGi has all the cool stuff."

He ruffled her hair. "We have cool stuff at the Sanchez house, too. If there's anything we're missing, I'll go buy it. Just give me a list."

"You can borrow any of my supplies," her mother offered, but Catalina knew he wouldn't accept anything from Laura Wimberly. He was such a good man, if he'd just let some of that pride fall away.

"Daddy, you have to come here and put it on this family tree. It's got everyone."

With narrowed eyes, he gave the tree a flat stare. The tension was back in his neck and shoulders. He glanced at the door.

He wanted to leave, but he was staying for Willa. Had he kissed her because he wanted her to stay in Port Del Mar with their daughter? Catalina was so confused she wanted to cry. Today had been a roller coaster of emotions.

And now her daughter would have two family trees. That's not what she wanted for her, but if she stayed here, how would she ever become an adult independent from her parents?

"Almost all done. We just need Paw-Paw's, Buelito's and yours, Daddy. Then it will be perfect." She looked over her shoulder. "Right, Mama? This is the best Christmas ever!" She clapped her hands, then started singing along with Noah. They all joined in when he started "Feliz Navidad," Willa singing at the top of her lungs. Then he switched to a quieter "O Holy Night."

Catalina was thankful that in her innocence Willa didn't realize there was any tension in the room.

Franny stepped away and, with a big smile, hugged her tight. "Thank you for pushing Andres to do this here with your father. It was a very special day." She leaned in closer and whispered, "Be patient with him. He's always had a clear idea of his responsibilities and how his life should go. There is also that mile-wide stubborn streak he gets from his father. He tries to hide it." She stepped back and squeezed her hands. "*Si Dios quiere.* Trust God's plan for you."

Trevor stood. "This has been fun, but we should start moving the boxes back up the old wobbly ladder." Her brother didn't sound very excited about his own suggestion.

Franny grabbed her arm and let out a soft gasp. "All of these beautiful Christmas decorations are gonna be put back in the attic?"

Catalina's mother nodded her head. "Many of these weren't even meant to come down. But with everyone it was easier to just bring them all. Some I'll never use again."

"Have you ever considered giving them away? It's such a shame for them to be collecting dust in a dark attic." Franny went to one of the boxes and lifted a heavy green garland with red and gold Christmas balls woven in with red ribbons.

"Oh, do you want them? You can have

those." Laura waved her hand over the large plastic boxes.

"We have our own," Andres mumbled. His mother shot him the mind-your-manners glare.

Turning back to Laura, she smiled. "Oh, no. Not for me. The sheriff's department leads a toy drive each year. Starfish Wishes. Andres is in charge of the booth they do at Christmas by the Sea. It's a new weekend event in Port Del Mar. They collect throughout the year, but that has become the biggest day for collecting donations. He has doubled the number of families they can help."

"That's wonderful." Laura clasped her hands in front of her.

"Mom." He sounded embarrassed.

"What?" His mother looked at him in all innocence. "You do so much but really, *mijo*. Your booth is a little sad compared to all the other decorated spaces along the boardwalk and plaza. This would look nice. And the extras can be given to struggling families."

"I didn't know you did a Christmas toy drive." It shouldn't surprise her. He had always looked out for those who needed help. That was the history of their whole childhood relationship. She had been a lonely little kid left on her own and he'd been there.

"It didn't start out that way. I was collecting soft toys that we could keep in our cruisers for children in traumatic situations. When you're dealing with kids, it's easier for everyone if you have something they can relate to and hold on to."

GiGi nodded. "Okay, decision made. I'll go through the vintage boxes and repack those. They are definitely staying on the ranch. You can take all the green bins. And the blue ones." She stood in the middle of the room with her hands on her hips. "What do you think, Catalina? Which ones should go?"

"Me?" Her mother was asking her opinion? "Are there any that have sentimental value?"

"Good question." She tilted her head and scanned the room. "Other than the ones you made and the vintage heirlooms, they were all bought by the designers. So, no. Take them all." She grinned. "There are so many boxes. Did you get everything you wanted, Willa?"

"I put the ones I liked on the tree." Her daughter was holding Andres's hand. "Do you need more toys, Daddy? I have more dolls and stuffed animals than I can sleep with."

He kneeled. "That is very kind of you. I imagine you could make a couple of kids happy."

"I'm donating, too, GiGi! We are going to help others. Then we can go to Christmas by the Sea and help Daddy make his booth beautiful."

"Yes. Then it's done. I feel so much better. Thank you, Franny. This was a great idea."

"Thank you for your generosity, Mrs. Wimberly." Andres's mother reached for Laura's hand and squeezed it.

Her mom waved her off. "Please, call me Laura. We do share a granddaughter."

"That's me!" Willa bounced between them. "I can help carry boxes."

Noah picked her up. "I think the boxes weigh more than you. Plus, your buelito took the SUV. They look too fancy to throw in the back of an old truck." He pushed at one with the tip of his boot. "I'm not sure they would all fit anyway."

"We have plenty of trailers on the ranch," Laura said. "Catalina, take Andres to the old Greyson barns. All the trailers are kept there. We'll move the boxes to the back carport."

With a tight smile Andres said thank you and marched out of the house. Catalina jogged to keep up with him, then scrambled into the cab as he started the engine.

The temperature had dropped, and it

was almost cold. "Sorry. I don't know why my mother sent me with you. You know where the trailers are kept, and I'm sure you've hooked up more than one by yourself."

She sighed and slumped against the worn bench seat. "Maybe she thought we needed time alone to talk. I'm sure Willa was the only one who was unaware we were fighting." She made herself stop rambling. They were alone and could discuss the job offer she might not even get. "I'd love to have a conversation, but that takes both of us."

She watched him and waited, letting the silence sit in the space between them.

Yeah. They needed to talk. But he didn't know what to say. He knew what he wanted to say, but that wasn't going to help.

"Has anyone mentioned that you have more pride than is healthy for a Christian man?"

He clenched his jaw because he knew

she was right. Her mother had just donated a trailer load of Christmas decorations and he was mad? "I believe the answer to that would be a big fat yes. Sorry. Your mother has been very generous. I'll make sure to thank her when we go back."

The sweetest smile was his reward. She touched his arm. "I appreciate that."

"Does she know you want to move to Canada?" His gaze stayed on the ranch road.

His voice was low and even. It was the kind of tone used to de-escalate a situation.

She relaxed. "It's not that I want to go to Canada. It's a career opportunity that I wasn't expecting. When I discovered I was pregnant, I thought all my dreams would have to be put away and I'd be dependent on my parents forever. When I found out that my supervisor recommended me, I was floored. That they're even considering me for this position is a huge deal. I'd be the youngest director. I really want the job, but it's not an easy decision."

He twisted his hand around the steering wheel as his knuckles went white. "Okay, but does your mother know about the job possibility?"

"Yes."

"Well, then, this makes sense. I'm useful to her now, because she wants me to convince you to keep Willa in Texas."

"Ugh!" Cat slammed her head back. "That's why she's being so cooperative. She's using you to get to me. My father probably put her up to it. They've been adamant about me not moving. If she tells your mother, I don't know what I'll do. I wouldn't be able to tell Franny no."

Arms wrapped around herself, Cat practically curled into a ball. "Please don't say anything. It might not happen. But if I get the offer, I don't want your mom to know before I make a decision."

Earlier, he'd been so wrapped up in his own feelings he hadn't seen her pain. Now it was as clear as a summer day without a cloud in the sky. "I read your letter."

"You did? Did it change any of your feelings?"

Her heart was in her eyes. Pulling up to the barn, he turned and drove through the wide doors in reverse. Parking, they sat there with just the sounds of the rattling engine.

"I made myself read it last night. I didn't want to. Reading the way you felt when it was happening scared me. I didn't want to feel sorry for you."

"Do you? Feel sorry for me?" Her beautiful face twisted in distaste. She had always hated pity. Preferring anger, she would push people until there was no sympathy left for the poor little Wimberly girl.

"You've always accused me of acting as if I know what's best for you. For everyone. And I've been guilty of that. But you have to realize it's the best way I know to take care of the ones I love. I protect people for a living."

"I know. But it doesn't make it easier to

take." She smiled and reached a hand out to him.

He pulled back. "In your letter, you were so worried about my future and my mother. My whole family. You worried about where we would live, about insurance and about how we'd make it without your father's support. You thought you were doing what was best for everyone."

"Looking back, I know I should have talked to you first, but I was scared. And my father... Well, he was always bigger than life."

"I know. And my pride can be an issue."

Her eyes went superwide. "Really? I hadn't noticed."

"Smart-mouth." They both chuckled. Then he sighed.

"I hate that my family was so dependent on the Wimberly ranch. Ever since the day you walked away from me and your father threatened me, I've worked hard to build a safety net. That was a situation I never wanted to be in again. If my family needed to leave the ranch, I would be able to provide for them. I didn't want anything from the Wimberly family."

"Oh, Andres. What about your future in the air force, at the academy? You never really told me what happened. I cut out pictures of fighter planes and pictures of your family happy. That's what I hung on to when I was scared and alone. Your mom's health and you living your dream of flying in the air force."

"That was never my dream."

"Yes, it was!" She straightened and leaned toward him. "All you talked about was flying. You built those models. Don't tell me anything else, because it would be a lie."

"I dreamed of flying, yes. I still do. The air force was my parents and your father. Since I did want to fly, I thought that was the only way to make it happen."

She sucked in her bottom lip and looked at him, tears hovering in her eyes. "I did what my father wanted to protect your dream. And it wasn't even yours? I'm not sure how I feel about that."

"Really? You don't know how you feel?"

She rolled her eyes at him. "Okay. I'm angry and frustrated, but I'm also confused."

"My family needed me. My community needs me. Where else would I be? I do fly. I've discovered that I love helicopters. I even fly for the ranch to get more hours, but it's just recreational."

"You have commercial licenses? Why don't you fly professionally?"

He gritted his teeth. How had this become a discussion about him? "Those are hard jobs to get without the experience. You have to start at the bottom and be willing and able to go anywhere at any time. I have responsibilities. I can't just run off and do whatever I want. And now I have a daughter. Are you teaching her that it's okay to leave whenever it gets tough?"

Withdrawing from him, she shook her

head. "No. You have some old hang-ups. I would do anything for Willa. Even moving out of the country if it means a better future for her. Leaving Texas is not easy, and it is not me running away this time."

She opened her door. "I understand that you have doubts about me. I'm sorry that taking this stuff from my mother is hard for you, but there is nothing wrong with accepting her offer. You've given me so much. It's okay to let others help to you."

She stood outside his truck and looked down. "This Christmas, everything is different. I want to be a different person. A year ago, I dedicated my life to God and promised to live in faith and honesty. Completing that vow has brought us home, so that Willa is with you and can be loved by the whole Sanchez family."

The door was halfway closed when she paused. Leaning in over the seat, she looked directly into his eyes. "I also want to be a good mom who raises a strong, independent little girl with love. I promise that no matter where I live, you will be in her life every day. Even if it means daily video chats as we get ready for the day and at night when she is tucked into bed. I will find a way for you to be involved."

He fought the urge to yell back that he wanted to be able to hold his daughter and swing her in the air. To smell the shampoo in her hair and hear her little heartbeat. None of that could be done over video.

But today had been too much of an emotional rodeo already, so he just nodded.

With a smile, she tapped the side of his truck. "Okay. Then let's get her hooked up."

Working together, it didn't take them long to connect the trailer. The large barn had a lineup of nearly a dozen trailers of all sizes and types for them to pick from. His family had used them back in the day when they traveled to stock shows and rodeos. The Wimberlys had provided for everything.

And he had resented it. It was petty, but he didn't know how to let that go.

In the truck, he turned on Christmas music. That always helped put him in a better mood. This year he had a daughter to share the season with.

He could understand Cat's need to stand on her own, but where did that leave him? Other than with feelings for a woman he should have never loved?

Chapter Ten

Willa pulled Cat along the Port Del Mar boardwalk. It was the first weekend for the Christmas by the Sea event and the whole town looked like a Christmas wonderland. It was even cold enough for jackets and scarves.

"Hurry, Mama. Come on, GiGi. Daddy said he needed help decorating his toy booth. He said GiGi gave him too much work and she should be the one to hang it all up." She grinned at her grandmother. "I told him we're good helpers. We are, right?"

Her daughter's excitement helped ease her nerves a little, but not much. On the ranch, she could pretend that they weren't the source of hot gossip in town. But now they would be seen together. Being stared at had made her do stupid things in the past. If they were going to watch everything, she did, she'd give them something to stare at. Now that she was a mother that philosophy sadly didn't work when she was trying to be a better person and a good role model for her daughter.

Franny had made things a little easier. She had told them yesterday that when people asked, she was saying that they had known about Willa all along, but that they didn't think it was anyone's business. Her mother now thought Franny was brilliant.

She was the best at stopping gossip.

"That's two and five! Twenty-five." Willa read the number spray-painted on a little flag. "Daddy said his tent was thirty."

"Sweetheart, slow down." Catalina's mother was trying to keep up and wave to people she knew. "Your father is not going anywhere."

Vendors were unpacking, turning the little seaside town into a perfect replica of the Victorian era. A few people gave her a side glance, but most smiled and greeted her. Christmas music rang through speakers hidden in trees.

"Oh, isn't this quaint. It's all new, you know. One of the De La Rosas' wives started this a few years back, but I hadn't come into town. It's like stepping into a Dickens novel."

"There he is!" Willa pulled away to run ahead.

"Willa, stay close to me. There are people unloading and moving around. Stay with me."

Andres stood with his hands on his hips, frowning at several of the Christmas boxes her mother had donated.

Cat waved. "Andres."

He looked up, the scowl firmly placed on his face. Then he saw Willa and his body language changed. The grumpy scrooge was gone, and the light of Christmas future shone.

In these moments, it was clear that coming home for the holidays had been the best choice. Hope for the future burned bright. Andres might never love her again, but all that love would fall on Willa.

At the corner of the Starfish Wishes tent, she let Willa go. Of course, she tackled Andres. "Daddy! We've come to help decorate and collect toys. Look! I brought Lilly." She lifted the floppy stuffed pony. "She is great for hugging. See?"

"She's perfect." He glanced up at Catalina. "Thank you so much for coming. I have no clue where to start. I usually just put out a green plastic table cover and a few red poinsettia plants around the donation boxes and call it good."

"Nonsense. You can never have too much Christmas." Her mother plopped her oversize bag on a table. "I have glue guns, hammers, tape and an electric drill. Where's the outlet for my power cord?"

She was looking around. "Melva told me there is a contest for the best decorated tents."

Catalina had no clue who Melva was. Her mother knew too many people for her to keep up.

"She said the nonprofits have their own category, and the prize is five hundred dollars—and, more importantly, a snowman's hat at the Tri-County Charity Christmas Snowball." She cut a glare at him. "When I told her that you would win this year, she laughed. She said the sheriff's department has never even tried to win. Of course, I was polite. I didn't tell her that this year you have me."

"A snowman's hat?" Andres looked at Catalina for help.

She shrugged. "The Snowball is a fancy dance and dinner that raises money for serval local charities. A great excuse to get all dressed up and show off."

Her mother rolled her eyes. "They spotlight five local charities. Each one gets a black top hat that people can put donations into. It can be a few thousand dollars on top of the other money raised during the event."

She lifted her chin. "And this year, you will have a hat." Laura plugged the glue gun in and held it up. "I hear there is going to be a new sheriff in town. You need to think about these things. It's good PR." She pointed a glue stick at him before placing it in the gun. Then all her attention went to organizing the Christmas stash and directing her helper, Willa.

"A new sheriff. What was that all about?" Catalina asked him, surprised to see him look embarrassed. "What's going on?"

"Merry Christmas!" The sheriff ducked under the canopy with a large cardboard box covered in red paper. On the side in gold glitter, it read Donations. "Mrs. Wimberly, I can't thank you enough for all your help. Sanchez here has been holding out on me."

Catalina could see Andres tensing up. Her mother laughed and hugged his arm.

She. Hugged. His. Arm. After checking to make sure her jaw was not on the ground, Catalina stepped closer to her mother. The woman was not picking up on the clues that Andres was tossing out. He did not want her hugging him.

Laura greeted the older man. "Sheriff McNay, I must say that I was sad to hear of your retirement. You've done such a great job, but I think you're very wise to hand the baton off to Andres. He's always been such a hard worker and takes his responsibilities seriously."

"Sheriff?" Did her voice sound as high-pitched to them as it did to her ears?

"Well, the people have to vote him in. But he's well respected." The sheriff glanced at her. "People understand we all make mistakes. Especially when we're young. But like you said Mrs. Wimberly, he takes responsibility. People like that."

Heat climbed her neck. *Mistakes.* Was

he referring to her or her daughter, or maybe both?

"Mrs. Wimberly." Andres gently stepped away from her mother. "I haven't even talked to my parents about the job. How did you know the sheriff had asked me to run?"

Laura waved him off. "It's a small town. Now, back to the plan at hand to get you more money. We wrap the poles with the garland that has the gold and red Christmas balls and these mini Mexican tin stars. I have several medium ones we can hang along the edge, then the three large ones can be placed on the end. You'll be surrounded by stars. It will do a great job of reflecting the Starfish Wishes theme and, with fairy lights tucked inside, it will represent hope and leading the way home."

Her mother sighed. "Everyone deserves a safe, warm home with plenty of food and hope. We should always have hope." She clapped, then went back to work.

Willa handed her large candy canes. Andres tied the huge red bows to the top of the four poles as she draped the ribbon along the edge.

Catalina leaned down to whisper to him. He was standing under her ladder. "Sheriff? Really? You don't think that's something you should have told me about?"

Adjusting the red ribbon about the banner, she tried not to stare at him as he attached the big bows.

"Hey, at least you know where I'll be. I'm not leaving the country. I haven't even filed to run."

"But if you're sheriff, I imagine you will have less time off. You can't be flying to Canada. You have to be close in case of emergency. You'll always be on call. Even when you're not."

He didn't say a word to that, which meant that he had either given up talking to her or that she had won and he didn't have anything to say back. The victory was hollow. She hated fighting with him. Always had. Her world just didn't feel right when he was mad at her.

"Andres," she whispered.

"Catalina!" She jumped at her mother's voice coming from behind her. "You know what? You should take Andres to the charity Snowball. Your father and I always attend. Wimberly Cattle Company is one of the Gold Star sponsors. Ha. Stars."

Laura dangled one of the large tin ones. "You can host the table and we can invite the sheriff's department to sit with us. Obviously, your father and I will not be going this year. It will be my first time missing it since we were engaged. Did you know it was right after our first Snowball that your father asked me to marry him?" Looking off in the distance, her eyes had a suspicious shine. Was her mother going to cry?

With a blink, her smile was back in place, but a little sadder. The hint of tears were gone. "In some ways it seems only a few years, but in others it seems a whole lifetime."

She glanced between Andres and Catalina. "You should go together."

"Mom." Catalina took a step down the ladder. "I'm sorry. But you know how much I hate these formal things. The talent for embarrassing you and Dad still burns bright in this one." She points to herself. "It's been years since I've gone."

"You used to work very hard to upset your father and me. You're a mother now and have outgrown that stage. You'll be fine. It will be great for Andres and his run for sheriff. You have to think about these things now. They impact Willa's future."

"Mrs. Wimberly. I'd rather not—"

"Stop." Her mother cut him off. "Andres, it is the best networking opportunity. People who can help make you sheriff will be there. So will the people you will be working with once you are in the office.

You have to go as our guest. It will help put any nasty rumors about us as a family to rest."

His jaw flexed. "I'm not going."

The sheriff laughed as he brought another box to the table. "You'll be going. If we get a top hat spotlight, the department has to be represented. Who better than you? You also have ties to the Wimberly name now." He leaned in closer. "It's a golden opportunity." The older man tipped his cowboy hat, then winked at Catalina before leaving again.

"You're about to drop that star," Andres called up to her.

"I have it. I just need a hook to put over the bar." Glancing down, she paused. She imagined Andres at the Snowball. He would look so good in a black tux, wearing his best Stetson and polished boots. They would love him.

Suddenly he was on the other side of her ladder. Reaching over her, he put a heavy

S-hook in place. "There. Can you lift it up high enough?"

Why was she suddenly short of breath? He smelled of fresh ocean air and bonfires on the beach. She leaned forward.

"Cat? Are you okay?"

She blinked up at him. "Uhm. Yes?"

He put a hand on her arm. "You look a little dizzy. Don't fall off the ladder. I'd have to do an incident report. I hate paperwork."

He was so close. With his other hand, he took the tin star from her and hung it, then reached inside the little trapdoor and turned on the fairy lights. The intricate design punched into the tin glowed from within.

The patterns played across his strong features. She felt all sorts of stuff she shouldn't be feeling.

"I have to admit that these really lift the level of Christmas spirit." He tucked a strand of stray hair behind her ear.

"Well, isn't this cozy?"

She jerked back, and Andres had to grab her to keep her from falling. Their math teacher stood below them. A very knowing smirk on her face.

"Mrs. Flores. How are you doing?"

Easing down the ladder, he managed to keep his hand on her shoulder. Until they reached the middle steps, anyway. The space was too big, and he dropped his arm. Without his warmth keeping her anchored, she felt adrift in the cold wind.

"Oh, me? I have my feet firmly planted on the ground." She chuckled at her own joke. "It's good seeing you together. Everyone else is acting all shocked. But I knew when y'all were in my class that there was more to you than just friends." She chuckled. "You had those goo-goo eyes for each other."

Heat moved from the center of her chest and up her neck. She didn't have to look around to know that everyone in the vicinity was watching them. In the past, this is where she'd do something outrageous to shock everyone and prove that she didn't care.

But she did care. She always had. She understood now that she had cared too much. Her fingers tightened around the rough wooden legs of the old ladder. She couldn't move.

"My, my. This must be the little girl everyone is talking about." Mrs. Flores moved into the booth.

Andres leaped down the last few steps and took Catalina's hand to help her down.

"You are a perfect mix of both your parents."

Andres let go of her and picked up Willa. With one arm protectively around their daughter, he reached for Catalina with the other. Her heart melted as she tried to catch her breath.

"I'm Willa and I am half Wimberly, half Sanchez."

"Yes. I can clearly see that. I taught your parents in geometry and calculus. They both were very smart in math, but your daddy was there every day and always did his homework, so he had straight As. Your mom was smart, too. She'd come in and score higher than everyone else on the test. They would get so mad at her. Everyone but your daddy."

"Catalina was good at math? Her grades were horrible." Her mother didn't have to sound so shocked. Catalina shot her a glare.

Mrs. Flores laughed. "Yes, her grades were atrocious. I didn't say she was a good student. I said she had a mind for math. Your parents are very smart people. Maybe one day I'll have you in math."

"I can count to one hundred."

"You are smart. Your daughter is precious. Be careful, time slips through your fingers faster than you can imagine." Mrs. Flores patted Willa. "Treasure her and spend as much time as possible letting her be a little girl."

"Yes, ma'am, that's the plan," Andres said, as polite as ever.

Chin raised, Mrs. Flores scanned the booth over her glasses. "Nice work. You've stepped up your game. I hear rumors you will be running for sheriff. The town needs more men like you."

"Thank you." He frowned. "But the sheriff hasn't even announced his retirement yet, so it's a little premature for that kind of speculation."

"He will be attending the Charity Snowball with Catalina," Laura announced. "We are hoping the booth does well enough to get the board's attention."

"Very good." Mrs. Flores nodded her head to her mother, then moved on to the next booth.

"Mother," Catalina said through clenched teeth. "What was that last part about? Why would you tell her we're going to the Snowball?"

"Her husband is on the city council and sits on the Tri-County Welfare Board. They pick the organization that gets the last hat. You have to know these things.

It's important in a small town. Well, in any town where you want to make things happen. Like running for sheriff."

Catalina tilted her head back and looked at the pretty stars they had just hung. "Mom, we don't need a debutante lesson on networking."

"Catalina, sometimes I forget how you were as a child. You want them on your side."

"My side?" He kissed Willa on the head. "You make it sound like we're gearing up for a fight. It's a charity ball. For charities."

Her mother tsked. "Oh sweetheart, it's so much more."

"What's a charity ball. Is it a game?" Willa asked.

Her mother reached for Willa. "It's a beautiful party where they serve fancy foods and sparkly drinks. A million lights are hung inside, and everyone dresses up to dance all night while raising money for those who need it."

"I want to go. I love dress-up and sparkly drinks."

"It's for big girls and boys. You and I can help your mama get all pretty, then we will have our own special party. Who would you want to invite?" They headed off to the back of the booth to finish the tabletop decorations.

Andres tapped the tip of the star above Catalina's head. "That wasn't too bad for our first public encounter together."

She snorted. "I'm pretty sure we didn't have goo-goo eyes for each other. At least not on my part. I knew that you were way out of my league."

"What? You're a Wimberly. I was the son of your dad's ranch hand."

She rolled her eyes and added more tiny stars to the garland wrapped around the pole. "The son of a foreman who managed the fifth-largest cattle company in Texas. He worked his way to the top of the ranch food chain and earned my daddy's respect. You were the best-looking boy on campus, class valedictorian, student council, starting quarterback, homecoming king and FFA president, which is the biggest deal in these parts of the world. I happen to know that people asked you all the time why you even gave me the time of day. Hanging out with me just proved how nice you were on top of it all. Everyone loved you. You were going places. I was the troubled youth."

"Wait." He leaned in closer. "You thought I was the best-looking boy at school?"

"Really? That long list of accomplishments and that's all you heard?" She tossed a random glitter-covered pine cone at him, then turned to arrange the donation boxes. Items had already been dropped off.

"I guess Mrs. Flores was more observant than we gave her credit for. This is one of the things I love about a town so small all the grades are on one campus. So what year was it that you started giving me goo-goo eyes? Let's see…" He squinted and twisted his mouth to the side, acting as if he was deep in thought. "My seventh-grade year I was in your eighth-grade algebra class. We had geometry together the next year." He followed her. "Or was it—"

"Stop being such a boy." She couldn't look him in the eye. She glanced over her shoulder. Where were Willa and her mother when she could use an interruption?

"But I am a boy." He shrugged with that I'm-so-proud-of-myself smile slanted across his face.

"No." She poked him in the chest. "You're a grown man. Act like it."

He trapped her hand in his. "I remember the minute I looked at you and knew I wanted more than friendship." The playfulness was gone. "But it happened earlier for you? When?"

"How do you know that? Maybe you had a crush on me first."

"Nope. Not if Mrs. Flores saw you giving me puppy-love eyes."

She pulled her hand free and slugged him. Truthfully, it was more like a tap. *I'm so pathetic.*

He leaned back on the table and crossed his legs. "You were always my favorite person to hang out with. Since you graduated a year before me, I agreed to go to the prep school. If we had been in the same class, I would have stayed and graduated with you."

"Really?"

He nodded. "The Air Force Academy was never my dream. When I came home for Christmas, you were in the kitchen with my mom and Eva. Y'all were singing 'Bidi Bidi Bom Bom' as loud as you could. Your hair was swinging around your face as you danced with them. You hair had one pink stripe. You looked up at me and your smile just…" He threw his fingers in the air. "Erupted. I was struck by lightning. Birds, stars, the whole cartoon-thing was happening in my head."

He paused. The brown eyes grew darker.

"I knew at that moment that you belonged in my kitchen. I had been missing home so much, but it had been you. I had been missing you the most. My funny, smart girl who saw the world in a way no one else did."

Her throat was dry. "I remember that day. When you walked in, my whole world shifted with the look in your eyes. You kissed me that night. A sweet, gentle kiss, but it told me everything I needed to know. You had finally noticed me. Those were the best weeks of my life."

"Yeah." He straightened and rolled his shoulders as if he'd been in the same position too long. "We were in a bubble, protected from reality. Your parents were in Houston and mine... Were gone a lot." He sighed.

Reaching out to touch his arm, she nodded. "We had no idea what was about to hit us. There should be warning signs in life. Danger—steep curve ahead."

He snorted. "Watch for falling rocks."

Scanning the area, he had his profile to her. She took the unguarded moment to study his face. He had always been a beautiful boy. Now his features were hard and strong in a way that made a girl believe he could take care of anything that came his way.

"What about you? Was it my sophomore year? You were a junior and we had Mrs. Flores for pre-calc. Was that when you fell madly in love with me?"

She puffed out her cheeks. "Love? I wouldn't go that far. And it was much earlier. It was when we had her for algebra."

He paused and his eyes went wide. "When I was a seventh grader?"

"We both know you were a very advanced seventh grader. Come on. You were taking a math class with eighth and ninth graders. It was at the first pep rally. You ran into the gym leading the junior high football team. Then you stepped up to the mic with all the confidence of a seasoned pro. You're a natural-born leader.

All the girls were going crazy over you. Then you winked at me. I knew it didn't mean anything, but you didn't care what anyone thought of our friendship."

"I thought the other kids were missing out. And your parents. I just didn't understand why you didn't show people the girl I knew."

"They didn't want that girl." Not knowing what else to say, she shrugged and moved to the next table. "You're going to make a great sheriff."

He groaned. "Not you, too."

She looked up from the centerpiece of pine cones, holly and strings of wooden cranberries. "What does that mean?"

"I just don't—"

Mrs. Flores called out to them, then waved from the funnel cake food truck. She pointed to the booth and gave him a thumbs-up.

"So, it seems as if I'm your prom date. It's a few years late, but if I have to go, I'm glad it's with you."

"Prom?" That came out way too loud and high-pitched. She glanced around and lowered her voice. "I've never even been to prom."

"I know. You were suspended, and then your parents grounded you. Consider this the prom you never got. I'm not going without you. I'll be so outside my element. It's more your crowd."

"Were you not there for my entire childhood and teen years? I don't fit in. I break all the rules."

He leaned down. "But you know the rules. That puts you one step ahead of me. Come on. Together we can do this."

She nodded. "Together." That sounded much better than it should. He was just talking about the Snowball. In the real world, they would never fit together.

Across the street, a couple of women she recognized quickly looked away when she made eye contact.

She pushed down the urge to stick out her tongue at them. Instead, she smiled.

See, she could be a grown-up. She just wished she could be with Andres. She stopped breathing.

Where had that thought come from? The hope of her and Andres ever being more than co-parents to Willa had no place in her thoughts or heart.

Even if she stayed in Texas, he had a future here as sheriff. Once again, she had the opportunity to ruin his future plans.

Nope. She couldn't allow her heart to go there.

Chapter Eleven

Carefully applying the mascara at the edge of her lashes, Catalina leaned closer to the mirror. Over her shoulder hung the classy black sheath dress her mother had found. It was…pretty and perfect for the Snowball event.

"Mama!" Willa ran under the short dresses hanging on one side of her closet, which was really more of a dressing room. It was bigger than Willa's whole bedroom in Austin.

Her daughter chatted about her daddy while investigating every drawer, shelf and box.

This morning, her supervisor had called to let her know that they would be offering her the job. A queasiness rolled through her stomach. She hadn't been able to eat since the call. Andres thought Austin was too far away for his daughter to live. Did she tell him tonight or wait until she had more info?

"You have so many pretty dresses." Willa twirled to the other end where the shelves of shoes went to the ceiling. "And shoes. Why do you have more shoes than you wear? I don't think I can even count that high."

She looked so little standing in front of the wall of shoes that her mother had bought for her over the years. "Tomorrow you can help me go through them. The ones I won't wear, we can donate." Which was most of them.

"Oh, Mama! These boots!" Willa pulled out a pair of tall cowboy boots. They were handcrafted white leather. "I love the tiny little flowers growing up the side."

"They were hand-embroidered. I wore them so much I had to have the heels replaced."

"You should wear them tonight!"

"They don't go with the dress I'm going to wear."

"Then you should wear another dress. And we live in Texas. PawPaw says cowboy boots are always appropriate. I can help you pick out another dress if you want. Daddy says I have great taste. I can pick one for you that will go with the boots."

Willa was quoting her *daddy* more and more. Her daughter loved having a daddy. Of course, Andres made it easy to love him.

She could kick herself for waiting so long to bring Willa home to the other half of her family.

Home. She had always loved the ranch, but this was the first time it had felt like home. Maybe it was all the Christmas feels, and after the new year it would go back to normal.

Tears hit her from nowhere. Why was she getting so emotional? Leaning closer to the mirror, she gently wiped the tear away, then touched up her mascara. "Straighten your makeup, girl." She could imagine what her mother would say. "Mama wouldn't approve."

A loud gasp came from the other side of the wall of shoes.

She stood. "Willa. Are you all right?"

Her daughter met her at the corner. She had found the ballet costume from her last show. Catalina had been going to wear it at the Houston performance her parents had pulled her from.

The last time she looked at the long tulle skirts she had cried, heartbroken not to be able to dance. Her parents hadn't understood how dance helped her.

The top was covered in silver sequins that trickled down the multiple layers of white tulle like snow falling on untouched ground. Could she even still wear it?

"Mama, you have a princess dress." Her

daughter's eyes were wide with wonderment. "You have to wear it. With the white boots. Daddy will fall in love with you."

She laughed. "Oh, sunshine, that boat left the dock long ago. Me and your dad are not getting back together. And there is also a possibility that this dress will not fit me anymore."

"But maybe it will. GiGi says anything is possible."

"There are some things that we have to leave up to God."

"Try it on, Mama." She lifted the dress as high as she could, but there still was more of it on the carpet.

Did she risk trying on the dress and it not fitting? More importantly, did she risk her heart with Andres? Life had taken them in different directions. Even if she stayed in Texas, she couldn't see the town being happy with her as local sheriff's wife.

She lifted the dress. For one night, she

could pretend to be in the stories she loved. Her own kind of Cinderella.

Andres adjusted his tie, even though it was already neatly tucked into his vest. He had decided to go with the cowboy tuxedo. He switched his black cowboy hat to the other hand and smoothed his tie again. He resisted the urge to look at his watch. It couldn't have been more than a few minutes, even though it felt as if he needed to shave again.

"You look really nice," Laura assured him. *Yeah, he was that obvious.*

Rolling his shoulders, he relaxed and smiled. "Thank you."

"Are you sure I can't get you anything to eat? Something to drink?"

"I'm good. Thanks."

She sat on one of the wingback chairs that created a cozy setting in a large space. He guessed that was the difference between an entryway and foyer.

"Calvin always ate a full meal before

we went to one of these things. The food served is hit-and-miss, and he spent most of his time talking anyway."

Through the archway, he could see the two trees they had decorated after Thanksgiving. He had added an ornament along with his dad and Mr. Wimberly. He grinned. It was a true joint Wimberly-Sanchez project. It gave him hope. There had to be a way to make this work.

Then his gaze moved to the fireplace and the almost life-size painting of the Wimberly family, minus Catalina. Krystal and Trevor were young, so Catalina hadn't been born yet.

"Why didn't you have another portrait done after Catalina was born?" That had always rubbed him the wrong way. More evidence that she wasn't really a part of the Wimberly family, but an afterthought they had to deal with.

Laura's gaze went to the painting. "Oh, you don't know the story behind that? Calvin's best friend growing up became an artist, despite his family's misgivings." She studied the painting for a long minute. "Greg was killed in a motorcycle accident before he delivered the finished portrait to us. If you look closely, you can see areas he was still working on. After the funeral, his parents brought it to us."

"I'm sorry." His mother was always telling him that everyone had a story. That changed the way he looked at this family portrait.

"You know Calvin. He doesn't talk about feelings or anything that might be messy. So, I just let it stay and never asked him if we should do another."

"Does Cat know the story?" To her, that painting was proof that she wasn't a real part of her family, just an accident that they would have been fine without. But this gave it a new narrative.

Mrs. Wimberly blinked at him as if it had just occurred to her that Catalina might wonder why she was never included in the family painting. "I... I don't know. She should. I'll make sure she knows."

Shifting his weight, he looked up the staircase. Really, what was taking her so long? Cat was never one to spend hours on her hair and makeup.

"Maybe I should go check on them. Willa is helping her, but we picked out a dress yesterday and I let her borrow a pair of my shoes that will be perfect with it. I promise she'll look really nice."

"She always looks nice." That might have been a little sharper than he intended.

"What a gentlemanly thing of you to say. But we both know that in the past she had gone out of her way to be as inappropriate as possible. I never understood how that happened. Krystal always made sure she looked just right for whatever event we had to attend. Did you know she keeps an extra outfit in her car and office just in case?"

"In case of what?" He frowned. "Cat and Krystal are two very different people." He wanted to say more, but it was not his place. He sighed and looked up again.

"You know Catalina was a complete shock. She is proof that no matter what we plan, God has his own ideas. She was so...much. I didn't know what to do. We had established routines and a life we really loved." She folded her hands in her lap.

"I know I made a lot of mistakes with Catalina. I fought battles I couldn't win. Come to find out, they weren't even worth winning."

She stood up and crossed the vast foyer into the living room, stopping in front of the fireplace. She tilted her chin up to gaze at the perfect family portrait that didn't include Cat. "Catalina was born rebellious. And then there are the learning problems. Both of my other kids, they just did what was expected. Everything in school came easy. I really thought I was a great mom. Turned out they were just good kids."

"Catalina was a good kid, too. She's just different from them."

"Yes. She has very much been her own person. She might be more of a Wimberly than anyone in the last few generations. They were a very stubborn, hardheaded group of people. They would have to be to build what they did out of nothing."

Turning to face him, Laura Wimberly smiled. "She is a better mother than I ever was. That might be because of your mother." She shrugged, as if downplaying the emotions this confession caused. "All I know now is that my world changed when I first held Willa in my arms. There is a love for a grandchild I can't even begin to describe. I get to start over with a clean slate. She has no preconceived notions of me. I'm her GiGi. I didn't know it was possible to love someone as much as I love that little girl."

He totally understood that.

She bit at her bottom lip. He'd never seen Mrs. Wimberly nervous. "You feel it, too, right? I would do anything to keep her in Texas. If there's anything I can do to make it easier for you to convince Catalina to stay here, or at least in Austin… Anything we could give you?"

He took a step back and scanned the living room walls. A couple of days ago, he would have agreed with her. Maybe even plotted a way to keep Cat and Willa in Texas. He looked up at the portrait. "I do want my daughter close to me, yes. But Catalina's future is at stake, too. It's a hard decision that Cat is taking very seriously. I don't think we have a right to manipulate her emotions because we want Willa in Texas. Do you really think Catalina would do anything that would hurt Willa?"

"No! Of course not, but she has a habit of jumping without looking. I know she's a great mother. But even good mothers can make mistakes. Believe me, I know that firsthand. It's selfish, but Willa is the best thing in my life. She loves me without expectations. It breaks my heart to think of her so far away."

Everyone can use someone who loves them, and with Calvin so sick, Laura had to feel adrift. But he had no clue what to tell her. Cat deserved her dreams, too. She had been working so hard to stand on her own.

And with that, the angst that had been twisting him every which way settled. He would support Cat in any decision she made. For years, her parents had tried to make her into what they wanted. He wasn't going to join their ranks.

Footsteps and giggling above them saved him from any more enlightening conversations with Laura Wimberly. The evening hadn't even started, and he had a headache.

His girls were finally coming.

His girls.

No. Just one of them was his. Sadness wrapped around his heart. Cat had grown up being an afterthought—if her family thought of her at all. Why hadn't he fought harder to get to her when she had left for California? She had never been anyone's priority. He was mad at her for abandoning him, but he had abandoned her, too. His pride and ego had gotten in the way of the truth.

"Daddy," Willa called from the top of the stairs. She was holding Catalina's hand. "Look at Mama! She's a snow princess!"

His gaze shifted from the new center of his world to... Not what he was expecting. His mouth and brain disconnected from words or any rational thought. All he could do was stare.

Her hair was up, but loose curls fell, brushing against her shoulders. She shimmered as she floated down the stairs. Elegance and grace. She was a walking dream. Her tall white leather cowboy boots played peekaboo through all the layers of skirts as she moved forward.

"Catalina Wimberly! What are you wearing?" Her mother rushed to the foot of the stairs. "Where's the black dress? And the silver shoes?"

There was a shift in Cat's posture, then she straightened her spine. It was subtle, but he saw it.

Willa jumped down the steps, her pink tutu flopping with each bounce. "I found one of Mama's ballerina costumes in the back of her closet. Which I must say is bigger than a football stadium. She said she never got to wear it. It's so beautiful. I told her I thought she looked like a snow princess. And did you see the boots?" She stopped halfway down the stairs and looked back up at her mom. "They are so much fancier than the other shoes."

Cat smiled at Willa. She stood a little straighter and started walking down the stairs. Her hand reached out and took her daughter's. "Mother, this year's theme is Winter Wonderland Fairy Tales. When Willa suggested I wear the ballet dress with the Western boots, I thought it expressed my style perfectly. We think it's beautiful. I love the way the skirt falls around the top of the boots." She fluffed the skirt around her and kicked a boot out to the side. "I really love the way this looks. It's romantic and Western all rolled together." She glanced at herself in the six-foot mirror on the opposite wall and twirled. "This is something I always wanted to wear."

He had been ready to ride in and save her from her mother, but she hadn't needed him to come to her rescue.

"Daddy, what do you think? She looks like a snow princess, doesn't she?"

He picked Willa up, swinging her high, then placed her on his hip. "I'm thinking she's the snow queen, because you are my perfect little snow princess."

He tickled her belly, and she giggled. He wanted to record that sound so he'd have it whenever he needed cheering up. She tucked her head under his chin and snuggled against his chest. "And you're her cowboy king."

Meeting Cat's gaze over their daughter's face, he smiled. A few of the red strands fell around her face. She bit her lip. "Is this okay? You'll be walking in with me. You look great, by the way. You'll have everyone there ready to support your run for sheriff. I can change—"

"No, Mama!" Willa yelled, at the same time as he shook his head. She slipped to the floor and ran to her mother.

"Don't you dare change." The corners of his mouth stretched into a grin. This was the real Cat. Whimsical, romantic and practical all rolled into one amazing package. He knew it was a goofy grin, but he couldn't stop.

"It's my pleasure to be going with the Snow Queen to the Snowball." He bowed, then with his free hand took hers and lightly kissed the back of her knuckles. Her skin was so soft and her fingers delicate in his rough hands. Still bending, he looked up and met her gaze. "You're gorgeous, absolutely stunning. Don't change a thing."

She lifted her chin, a higher confidence settling over her shoulders.

"GiGi, don't you think Mama is beautiful?"

Cat laid a hand on Willa's head. "It's okay, sweetheart. People have different tastes and styles."

Laura went to Cat and hugged her. "She's beautiful. Give me your phone and I'll take a picture of you. All three of you sparkle tonight."

Willa laughed. "Daddies don't sparkle. They are strong and handsome."

"I'd say that with you and your mom by my side, I might shine a bit brighter."

After a few pictures in front of the tree, Andres glanced at his watch. "Time to head to our carriage. We need to hit the road."

"Ouch! That sounds painful." Willa giggled.

He took his keys out of his pocket.

Laura went to the desk and opened a drawer. "You should take one of our vehicles. The black Escalade would look nice."

"Thank you." He stiffened. When would Laura Wimberly stop seeing him as a charity case? "My truck works fine."

Laura made a face. "Are you sure? It's at the—"

"Mom." Cat joined him and took his hand. "We're going in Andres's truck."

"Okay. Do you need gas money?"

He bit back a growl. *Really? He was an officer of the law.*

"Mom!"

"What?" Her mother sighed. "I was only trying to help. I'm not saying another word." She waved them off and took Willa's hand. "You two have fun. Willa, PawPaw and I will be having our own party, so stay out as long as you like. No hurrying back."

Willa pulled away from her GiGi and jumped at Andres. Leaning in, she whispered loud enough for everyone to hear,

"Make sure to kiss her under the full moon. That's what the king does on a special night like this."

"Willa." She could feel the heat climb her neck.

Andres laughed it off. "How about I kiss my princess good-night?"

And with last kisses, they headed out the door to the ten-year-old blue truck waiting in the front drive.

Hand on her back, he helped her step up into his truck. He took a deep breath to control the sudden flash of connection. His heart lurched. No, he couldn't confuse the situation with developing feelings for her all over again. There was too much on the line.

Tucking her skirts safely inside the truck, he closed the door and walked around the back. He needed that little bit of extra time to collect his thoughts and emotions. Tonight, he would start the subtle campaign for sheriff. This was to show everyone that they were friends and co-parents.

No drama here, folks. Inside, he gave her a nod and started the engine. *No drama.*

In the cab of his truck, Catalina played with the edging on the tulle skirt. "Sorry about that. She doesn't mean anything other than she thought she was helping. It's just the way she thinks."

He gave a noncommittal grunt.

As they crossed over the bridge, the Texas sky stretched across an endless landscape. Running her hand along the door, she smiled at all the memories.

Between the possibility of her moving to Canada and him becoming sheriff, they had so much to talk about. Now that her boss had confirmed they'll be offering her the job, she was out of excuses to tell him.

She was a coward if she didn't tell him sometime tonight.

"Loyalty and commitment make up

your backbone. That's one of the things I love the most about you."

He gave her a side-eye. "Where did that come from?"

Her eyes went wide. She had said *love*. "I didn't mean to say love. I meant that—"

He laughed. "I was talking about my backbone. Calm down."

"Andres Guillermo Sanchez. Did you just tell me to calm down?"

He rolled his eyes. "Guilty. Sorry. Freak out. Lose it. Come unglued. Have at it. Whatever you want."

Smiling, she leaned back. She tilted her head, looking at him. "That was the thing with you. I could always be myself and do whatever I needed to process what was happening at school or with my family. When I left, I didn't have anyone I could talk to." She shrugged. "Maybe that was a good thing, because I learned to deal on my own."

"Are you now saying I was an enabler?"

"You're a caretaker. You do whatever

others need from you. Whatever they expect." She paused. "Andres, do you really want to run for sheriff?"

"Of course. It's an honor. I can't turn this opportunity down." He slowed the truck and turned into the driveway for the event center. All along the curved path, hundreds of lights were arranged in cone shapes to look like Christmas trees. People were walking through them, taking pictures.

The white, gold and blue lights reflected off everything. She couldn't help but stared in awe. "It's so lovely."

A man wearing a Santa hat and holding a flashlight waved them through the grassy parking lot. "Wow. There are a lot of people here. The regular parking lot is already full."

Once they'd parked, he came around and opened the door for her, then held out his hand to help her down. She hesitated. It seemed too intimate and personal.

"Cat? Are you okay?" He was looking at her with concern.

She nodded and took his hand. It was warm and fit perfectly around hers. How did such a simple touch create so much chaos in her nerves? "Thank you."

Stepping down, she avoided any eye contact. He didn't let go of her hand as she moved forward.

"Cat, you're beautiful. Are you nervous? I know the gossip has been harder on you. It's unfair. We both—"

"It's okay. It's not your fault. I expected that. Anyway, you're the golden boy they all love." She stopped and made a point to look up at him. "I'm…good. Really. It's not the people that have me acting weird." It was him. And all the feelings that were rekindling. And Canada.

Her stomach lurched. She needed to stay in the moment and enjoy tonight. "Thank you for…well, for being you. You've made this homecoming so much easier. I know it's been a shock and you were angry.

You're probably still angry, and you have every right. If I could do it over, I'd be braver. I'd come to you right away."

"If I'd been braver, you would have never been alone."

He closed the distance between them. Or maybe she had, but they met in the middle, and gently their lips touched.

Chapter Twelve

Oh, that should not have happened. He pulled back and shoved his hands into his pockets. The stars above gave him a great focal point. He needed to clear his head. He also needed to say something. A kiss like that couldn't be ignored. Or maybe it could.

"Andres?" Her voice was low, but it hit him like a wrecking ball.

He cleared his throat and looked at his boots. "Sorry. Everything is so upside-down. We really shouldn't go down that road again." He should look her in the eye. Being a coward didn't sit well with him.

"There's too much at stake right now, and this would just make it messy."

She pulled her shawl tighter around her shoulders. He fought his instinct to wrap her in his arms. That would just send all sorts of mixed messages.

With a nod, she gave him a small smile. "We're here to show everyone that there's no gossip worth talking about. Kissing in the parking lot might not help our cause. I agree. This isn't a good idea. We aren't teenagers anymore. We need to be smart."

Nodding was all he should do. No more touching or comforting. The anger was gone, leaving a deep sadness in its place.

He studied Cat's profile in the moonlight. She had walked away from him. She was different now, but what if it got hard again? "The one and only time I thought I'd found my forever girl. It didn't end well. Took me a while to get over it." The jury was out that he had moved on at all. He adjusted his tie. "I can't afford to go there again right now."

She frowned and her hands fisted. "Who?"

"Seriously?" Was she messing with him, or did she really not know how much he had loved her back then? Had he not made it clear? Scanning his memories, he tried to recall when he had told her he loved her. He realized he'd never said the words.

She dropped her arms and her eyebrows squished together.

"You were the only girl I loved."

"Me? I'm confused. We had that two weeks before...well... I mean we flirted and went to the movies, but did it really mean that much to you?"

"I think you and Mrs. Flores were onto something. We started way before that week. That night I came to you was because I loved you and needed you."

She spun to fully face him. Her eyes wide with shock.

Did she not know? Had he been that closed off?

"How? You... I never..." She shook her head. "That night you had devastating news. We were so scared. It wasn't because you loved me. You cried. We both needed to hold on to someone, and it got out of hand. But it wasn't because... How was I supposed to know you thought I was your forever girl?"

Stepping closer, she poked her finger in the center of his chest. "You hate everything with the Wimberly name on it. I'm everything Wimberly. I always wanted to stay around you as long as you let me, but I never thought you saw me as anything more than temporary. How could I be your forever girl? I'm not anyone's forever girl."

He opened his mouth to say something, but nothing came. She was right about one thing. As a Wimberly, he hadn't thought she would really stay with him. He was the temporary one.

When she'd left, that's what he had expected from her. He didn't fight hard enough. He had gone to the house, had called, but he should have spoken to her himself. Gone to California to talk to her face-to-face. That would have been the only way to know the truth. But he had let his hurt pride win.

"Deputy Sanchez?" A female voice came from the dark.

He turned. "Mayor De La Rosa. Hello." He shook her hand, then turned to her husband. "Hi, Xavier. Beautiful night."

"It couldn't be more perfect," the mayor agreed. "Catalina. I'm so happy you came tonight. It's been a while, and your parents have always been great supporters of our community. I'm glad to see you both here. This is your first time, right?"

He nodded. "Yes, ma'am."

She tapped his shoulder. "Stop with all the formality. Please, just call me Selena. From what I hear, you'll be our next sheriff. You have our full support." She took her husband's hand. "Do you want to go in with us, or will you be staying out here a little longer?" There was a twinkle in her eye.

How long had they been out here? Had

they seen the kiss? He sighed, then turned to Cat, his arm out. "Are you ready to go?"

Cat laid a graceful hand on his sleeve. "Thank you for the offer. We would love to go in with you."

"Good. Andres, I'll introduce you to anyone who's not aware that you should be our next sheriff."

They followed the mayor and her husband into the historical building. His brain swirled with thoughts as he walked next to Cat.

Selena and Cat talked about the group of kids she had been dancing with and the performance they had planned for the Christmas by the Sea festival.

Without knowing it, she had become a part of the community. Why couldn't she just stay?

Catalina smoothed the layers of her shimmering tulle. Her boots gave her strength. Walking up the grand staircase next to Andres was like entering a winter wonderland. The steps led them to ornate doors that opened to a foyer. Patterns from hundreds of lit tin stars danced across every surface. Everything shone with silver and gold glitter. Her hand tightened on his arm as they stopped at the top of the landing.

She was thankful for Selena's invitation to walk in with them. She had to grin. Her mother had disapproved of the De La Rosa family. Now they were introducing her at the Snowball. She loved the irony of it all.

The ballroom sparkled, and she spotted several women wearing ballerina-inspired gowns. She wasn't as much of an oddball as she believed. She loved it. Music and laughter swirled around her.

Andres leaned down and whispered. "Are you ready to have fun, queen?"

She nodded. There was so much going on in her head that she was worried she would do something stupid. Of course, she was who she was, and she was always on the edge of doing something stupid. But she couldn't afford to mess up things with Andres. Or to start falling in love with him again. Or at least let him know she was having those feelings. She just needed to get her heart under control.

They took a few steps down into the grand room. Selena led them over to a group of people and made an introduction. Everyone was pleasant and chatted about Christmas, the upcoming festival and Starfish Wishes. Tension eased from her muscles and she relaxed for the first time since getting into Andres's truck. She smiled and made small talk.

Showing up with Andres had caused a little stir, but not the big splash she'd been afraid would happen.

They moved on to another group of friendly people. They asked about her mother and how her father was doing. It all seemed so normal and grown-up. There were a few glances that burned with questions, but no one asked them.

Her mother had been right, of course. Coming here with Andres was a good move. Everyone would see they were friends. There was nothing to look at or talk about.

The MC asked everyone to make their way to the tables. Her brother came in late and hugged her from behind. "Sorry. I got caught up with a call. How is everything going?"

"Really good. Better than I anticipated."

"I told Mom this was a good idea. Cut off any speculation. I had planned to be here for you both."

"No worries. We're big kids."

Trevor shook hands with the business associates who had been invited to sit at their table and introduced Andres as the future sheriff. He already knew a few of them.

While dinner was being served, she had a hard time keeping her gaze from wandering to Andres. She had so much to make up for after doing him wrong on so many different levels.

The details of the night when his mother had told him she had cancer were so vivid in her mind. At times, they would run in a loop, keeping her up at night. They had been facing losing the most stable person in their young lives. Their world had crashed, like a ship running into a rocky shore without lights.

He was right. They had hurt each other, and with Willa and their parents trying to find a good balance, this was the worst time for them to make their mess even more complicated.

But then again, they had been best friends. And she was a different person now. He was running for sheriff, and she had a job opportunity in Canada.

Willa, his parents, her parents, their jobs… It was all too much. She wanted to face-plant in the chicken and green beans in front of her.

But, she had to stay focused on the reasons she had come to Port Del Mar. One was that her father, for the first time in his life, needed her. And the second was so Andres could build a relationship with his daughter, before she left Port Del Mar.

Those were her commitments. Reconnecting to Andres on any other level would be wrong.

There couldn't be anything between them. Casual talk about the holidays, the weather and fishing floated around her, and she just smiled and nodded. Questions about Starfish Wishes came up, and Andres became animated explaining the work they did and the families they served.

The waitstaff started removing the plates. Selena De La Rosa invited a spokesperson from each organization benefiting from tonight's efforts to come up and share.

Andres looked so handsome in his jacket and cowboy hat. When he told the stories of the families they helped through Starfish Wishes, there were a few tears in the audience, hers included. She'd never been so proud. He was a really good man. More than she deserved.

On his way back to the table, he was stopped several times. He'd progress a few steps, only to be stopped again. At one point his eyes met hers. She knew that look. It was time to dive into the shark-infested waters and pull him out.

Mrs. Johnson, one of her mother's society friends, had cornered him. She was a woman her mother said never to trust. She had her hand around his arm, and Catalina could almost see the claws biting into his flesh. The woman had brought her daughter into the conversation.

Catalina came up next to him and smiled her best Wimberly smile. "Mrs. Johnson. Vanessa. My mother wanted me to tell you hi and that she missed seeing you."

There was more small talk, then Catalina turned to Andres. "You said there was a silent auction item you wanted to show me."

"Yes. I think Willa would love it." With

a polite nod, they left and made their way to the line of tables full of items people had donated for the auction.

"Thank you for saving me," he whispered in her ear. "I couldn't stand another minute of shallow smiles and polite chit-chat."

She laughed. "My mother trained me for this battleground."

Rows of people were signing their names on items, each hoping to outbid the previous person. She was amazed at the mountain retreats, beach getaways, artwork, jewelry and sports tickets people had donated to raise money for organizations that served the community.

Tomorrow she'd look into ways Willa and she could help others. It was so easy to stay in her safe bubble.

Scanning one of the auction sheets that contained two pages of signatures, she saw Andres's name. It was a helicopter ride over the Wimberly Cattle Company and along the beach. "You donate your time and Daddy donates the helicopter? That's so cool. I'm impressed."

He gave her that lopsided grin. "You're easily impressed. I'll take any chance to fly."

"Yes. But it's my dad. I didn't know you worked together on anything."

He shrugged and signed his name to a basket from a local bakery. "It's for a good cause, and not many people have access to the helicopters your dad owns. And it gives me airtime that I don't have to pay for. I'm close to two thousand hours."

"That sounds like a lot."

He put his hand on her back and guided her through the people lined up along the tables. Casual greetings and a few Merry Christmases came their way. She smiled as he kept them moving.

"It's what you need to get the big jobs," he said.

"Like what?"

"Fire, EMS, any transport. Two thousand is a minimum requirement for most of the higher-paying jobs."

"Is that what you want to do?" She stopped and looked up at him.

"Doesn't matter. I can't if I run for sheriff." He gazed over her shoulder, scanning the crowd.

He claimed it didn't matter, but he obviously didn't want to talk about it. That told her it did.

A local band took the stage and music filled the air. People moved to the dance floor. She took his hand and led him to the backdrop set up for photos.

A small group was walking away, so she pulled him over. They posed in front of the sheer curtain with a million lights and glittery snowflakes. Twisted greenery stood tall on either side. "We have to take a picture for Willa. She'll love this."

At the mention of their daughter, he grinned. Several pictures were taken.

The band went into a new song, and she swayed to the familiar tune. It was one she had heard hundreds of times in his mother's kitchen. "I love that song."

Without asking, he took her hand and headed to the dance floor. "If they're playing a Christmas cumbia, we have to dance."

Everyone started moving in a circle as the Latin rhythm carried them along. He swayed to the music, taking a step to the side, then one forward. He took her hand and twirled her under his arm, then swept her to his other side. She pulled away, smiling. He caught her hand and pulled her back to him. His grin was infectious.

Dancing, they moved forward, sliding in short steps side by side. Then he spun her again and led her to his other side. She loved the push and pull of the cumbia.

Joy bubbled up inside her as they swayed to the beat. She had to laugh as he twirled her across the dance floor.

Their friendship had always been the best thing in her life. The relationship they had had when they were younger was so much like this dance.

Despite all the obstacles, could they have more than friendship? His hand slipped from hers as they turned and made another lap. He winked at her.

She shook her head. What was she doing? The music and sparkling lights had brought on this wishful thinking. Just like those two weeks over the holidays, their little bubble would burst when the real world set in and everything fell apart.

But what if they got it right? Could she be a sheriff's wife? She shuddered at the thought of all that public scrutiny. All the options in front of her had her heart pulled in so many directions. Where did God want her? The lightness of the dance was buried under heavy doubt.

Living in faith meant she wouldn't always understand the places God put her. She didn't understand his plans. One last spin and the world blurred.

She didn't want to make the wrong decision. Not just for herself, but for Willa and Andres.

The song faded into something more modern, and he led her back to their table. Leaning in toward her ear, he said, "That was fun."

She nodded. "It was like we were back in your mom's kitchen. Not a care in the world. Those were some of the best times in my life." Her heart was beating a little faster than it should.

"We didn't know how good we had it." He pulled her chair out. "Now we get to eat cake."

Two chocolate snowflakes dusted with gold and silver sat on top of a red velvet cupcake. Taking a bite, he popped a piece of the snowflake in with the cake. With a quiet groan, he rolled his eyes. "I'm not sure what we were so worried about. This evening isn't so bad. Probably because we're doing it together. You always made the worst chore better." He took another bite. "Not that this part is a chore."

Trevor leaned over to see around Andres. "So, how did the phone call with Canada go?"

Andres dropped his cupcake. "You heard from your employer?"

The anger she had seen in his eyes the first few days after her arrival was back. The cream cheese frosting and chocolate topping soured in her stomach.

She wanted to hit her brother. Not that it was his fault. This was not what she wanted to talk about tonight. "Just my immediate supervisor. She called to tell me that it sounds like they are going to make me an offer, but I didn't want to say anything yet. It's not official."

Andres dropped is head, then after a big sigh he looked up at her. "I don't want to fight tonight, but I thought we were going to be open and honest going forward. If she told you that, then why wouldn't you talk to me?"

She gritted her teeth. He was right. She had messed up again. "It's not the real offer. They might not even call me until after the holidays. The job wouldn't start until the middle of January. I was going to sleep on it and talk to you tomorrow."

"Would you think about staying here if I asked you to?"

Tears burned at the back of her eyelids. She bit down hard on the soft skin inside her cheek to stop them from falling. She didn't know what to say.

Trevor cleared his throat, breaking the heavy silence that had fallen between them. "Sorry I brought it up. I know it would be a huge opportunity. Proud of you, little sis." He nodded to the table with the black hats. "It looks like the top hat for Starfish Wishes is close to full with donations. I'll go add my two cents." He made a quick exit.

Andres pushed his dessert back and stared at the people on the dance floor.

She hated being shut out. Even when she caused it. "Andres, I—"

"If we don't want the night to end in a fight, we probably should drop it."

"Okay." She stood. "I'm going to… I'll be right back."

"It's easier to run and hide, isn't it?"

"When you refuse to talk to me, yes." Not making eye contact, she turned and left.

In the hallway leading to the bathroom, Catalina found a little tucked-away nook with two wingback chairs. She needed to catch her breath and refocus her thoughts.

Maybe she could turn down the job. She could keep doing what she was doing in Austin. She wouldn't be able to get ahead, but maybe that wasn't the best thing for Willa right now.

If she put away her pride and was truthful with herself, she might as well move to Port Del Mar. She shuddered at the thought of moving back into her parents' home.

She had her condo in Austin. Why couldn't

she get her own place here? They didn't have to live at the ranch.

Moping about it was wasting time. She just needed to talk to Andres and get his opinion. If they were to be true co-parents, then he had a say in Willa's future.

The last time she had left and made all the decisions. Now she would do it differently. She'd talk to him about all the options. Make a list of pros and cons.

Taking a deep breath, she centered her thoughts and whispered a prayer. "God, my heart is open to your plans. My mind is open to your wisdom. I ask that your words are spoken, and I put my pride and desires aside." Hands on the arms of the dark green chair, she pushed up.

"I can't believe that he actually came here with her." It was Mrs. Johnson.

Catalina froze. Could she live in a town where half of the population still saw her as a troubled youth, a lost cause?

She eased back into the chair. The

woman had served on several of the same boards as her mother. But it had been all about social standing, not about the charities.

Did she step out and let them know she was here? She didn't want to face them right now, but they were between her and the ballroom.

"Do you really believe that he knew the whole time? She could be scheming him." A voice she didn't recognize sounded too happy at the nasty thought.

"Have you seen the little girl? I believe Franny's story. Andres is such a good man that he wouldn't do anything to hurt her, and the Wimberlys think so highly of themselves. They probably wanted to hide the connection. What I can't believe is that she managed to pull him into her life like that. She's always causing trouble. Not a thought in her head."

Squinting her eyes, Catalina concentrated. She knew that voice, but couldn't come up with a name.

"Not any good ones, anyway." They all giggled. There had to be four or five women.

"That little girl would be better off with him."

"He's so sweet and noble. I mean, he's stepping up and doing the right thing. That little girl is fortunate to have him."

"I, for one, believe that this puts doubt on his ability to be sheriff." Mrs. Johnson again. "I mean, having a child with her does cast a shadow on his ability to make good choices. He did date my Vanessa for a while last year, but he broke it off with her. I'm sure it had to do with Catalina Wimberly. She's just too spoiled and self-centered. And did you see her outfit tonight? What is with those boots with that dress?"

How did her mother smile and chat with these women, then later tell Catalina how much she disliked them? She wasn't made of the same stuff as her mom. She couldn't pretend these people were her friends.

"I kind of liked the mix. Very Texas chic." A new voice whispered, as if afraid to draw the queen's wrath.

"She thinks she's better than us. I'm Catalina Wimberly and I'll wear whatever I want and take whoever I want." There was a loud snort and more giggling.

"I hope she goes back to Austin soon. Hopefully she's just here for the holidays. Andres doesn't need this kind of distraction while running for sheriff."

Mrs. Johnson added to the fire that burned in Catalina's gut.

"We all know what a great guy he is. He'd be perfect for sheriff."

"Poor man did always have a weak spot for that youngest Wimberly." Mrs. Johnson was taking over the conversation again. "Remember when they were in school? He was always defending her. I never understood it. Of course, she had been kicked out of five other schools. And then the dance team. My Vanessa made sure of that."

"Vanessa lied. And it was three schools," Catalina said, under her breath. And she hadn't been kicked out. Her parents had moved her, looking for a better fit.

"Well, my Vanessa was good for him. She would be understanding and take in the poor little girl before it's too late. Her daughter will be just like her if he doesn't take over. How many schools do you think she'll be kicked out of?" There was more giggling.

She hadn't wanted to make a scene, but they'd gone too far. Now they were talking about her daughter.

Stepping out of the nook, she pulled out her mother's best social smile. The four women turned to look at her. She recognized two as old classmates.

When they realized who she was, there were different levels of embarrassment. "Hello, ladies." She smiled and waited a moment. They didn't say a word.

"I had promised my mother I would avoid making a scene, but when you started talking about Andres and my daughter, I had to step out. It brings to mind this morning's devotional. I thought I'd share. The focus was Proverbs 10:18. It said something along the lines of... 'And he that uttereth a slander is a fool.' Now, I would never call any of you fools. You're too smart and kind for that. Have a good evening."

The door to the courtyard was behind them. Walking around them, she paused. "And we agree on one thing. Andres Sanchez would make an excellent sheriff."

With the most graceful nod she could manage, she turned her back on them and walked down the corridor, the very long corridor, with her head high. She was shaking, but she had managed to stay calm and even smile at them. Her mother would be proud.

She didn't have the energy to go back into the ballroom and face everyone. They had all been so nice to her, but were they talking behind her back or was it just this little group? Was it possible she had misread the whole room?

Some of what they said was true. If she stayed in town, she'd be nothing but a distraction for Andres.

A couple of women she didn't know walked past her and smiled a greeting. She smiled back, hoping she was able to hide the acid burning in her gut. Did these women talk about her, too? What she hated most was that she was allowing a few women to make her feel like a socially awkward teen again.

She had to get outside. Fresh air. Space. She needed those. Well, if she was honest with herself, the list was much longer, but right now she had to get out of the building.

Opening the glass door, she entered another wonderland. Old oak trees were wrapped in lights. Ropes of golden sparkles hung from the sweeping branches, gently swaying in the breeze. Shrubs were flocked with fake snow, and red ribbon covered the posts on the pavilion.

Her boots couldn't get her to the little sanctuary fast enough.

Chapter Thirteen

Andres glanced at the archway Cat had disappeared through. He tried to focus on the words Parker Hernandez was saying, but Cat had been gone too long. Something was wrong.

Or was he being overprotective and paranoid?

"The fishing has been great this year. I tell you. This is the best life. Are you sure I can't convince you to join me? You love flying and you're a natural."

Parker was a part-time flight instructor at the local airfield. He also owned several recreational fishing boats, but he was gone during the summer months fighting fires as a helicopter pilot.

"Like I tell you every year, I can't go running off four months out of the year to play hero for someone else. I have a home and responsibilities."

Parker took a sip of his drink. "So the rumors are true? You're running for sheriff?"

"That's the plan." He glanced at the exit again.

"Congrats. That's a huge honor." Parker tucked his business card into Andres's chest pocket. "Call me if it doesn't work out."

"This is where I belong. My family's here." Most of them, anyway. He needed to find Cat.

Parker tapped Andres's shoulder. "You're not going to call me, are you?"

"Probably not."

Trevor joined them. "Sorry to interrupt, but I need to talk to you."

Parker excused himself.

He turned to Trevor. "What is it? Where's Cat? Is she okay?"

Trevor shrugged. "I'm not sure. My friend Brenda saw her outside the ladies' room and said something looked off. Then Cat practically ran out the back. She thought I might want to go check on her. I figured if she needs to talk to someone, she'd rather it be you. She clams up around me."

"The courtyard in the back?" Andres was already heading that way. He should have listened to his gut. He knew tonight was loaded with risk, but everything had been going so well.

Other than kissing her. And getting mad when he heard that Canada had called. Okay, but other than his mood swings, it all seemed like a great time. He scanned his memories for details he hadn't taken enough notice of.

She had been upset at his reaction to the mention of the call. Being out of sorts, he had accused her of running away. Is that what she was doing? But where would she go? They were in the middle of nowhere. He had his truck keys in his pocket, but she had hot-wired a car before.

Pushing open the door, cool air hit his face. The temperature had dropped, and he knew she wasn't wearing anything to keep her warm.

The area was covered in Christmas lights and fake snow. Walking down the brick path, he scanned the trees. White tulle stuck out from a tall shrub surrounding the pavilion. "Cat?" Not sure if it was her, he eased around to the front.

He heard sniffling. "Catalina?"

She stood and wiped at her face. "Andres. How did you find me?"

"A friend of Trevor's saw you come out here and was worried. He thought it would be better if I came to find you."

He hated seeing this strong, creative woman reduced to tears. "What happened? I'm sorry what I said about you running away. We can talk about Canada tomorrow. It was just a knee-jerk reaction. You know, me being a jerk. That's what my sisters tell me, anyway."

She made a strange sound, like a laugh combined with a gagging sound. She sat down and fluffed her skirt. "You? No. It's me. You could be sheriff." She waved at the historic hotel. "They all love you. You've always been the town hero."

Something inside him cried out that he wanted to be her hero. She rubbed at her bare forearms. Cautiously making his way to her, he slipped off his jacket and dropped it over her shoulders.

He didn't even bother to ask if she was cold. She'd shrug him off, not wanting any help. They both had an overabundance of pride and stubbornness. Their poor daughter.

Sitting on the edge of the bench next to hers, Andres nodded to the building behind her. "Most of those people in there don't even know me."

"What's it like to be loved by everyone?" She looked him in the eyes.

There was no drama or self-pity. She looked curious, the way she did whenever she learned something new on the ranch.

"I'm not sure what you're talking about." He was stalling because he knew very well what she was talking about, and it broke his heart. But the last thing she wanted was his pity.

With a sigh, she turned to the trees around them. The golden light highlighted her face and reflected in her eyes. For a moment, he couldn't catch his breath. For him, nothing compared to her beauty. It radiated from her, not in a traditional way, but from deep within.

She shrugged as if the question was not the saddest thing she had ever uttered. "I guess when it's all you've ever known it just seems normal. So you can't really explain it. Like asking me about being a Wimberly. Or being the talk of the town. It's just what my life."

She played with the lining of her skirts. "Some people think being a Wimberly makes everything easier. In a lot of ways, I guess it does, but in others it can be a heavy burden."

Pulling his jacket closer, Cat huddled inside it. "I guess being loved by everyone has its hardships, too. There are so many expectations. From the town, your family. Even people who don't know you."

"Cat." He scooted closer and took her hand, holding it still between his. Her skin was cold. This was more than what had happened between them. "Who said something to you?"

Her back straightened and her chin tilted up. He recognized that look. It was her go-to mask when she wanted to prove to the world that it didn't matter what anyone thought of her.

Oh, baby girl. He wanted to take her in his arms and hold her until all the hurt was gone. Moving closer, he reached for her face. "What happened?"

Pulling back, she stood. "Nothing. I just needed fresh air."

"I'm not buying that. I know that look. Someone has done something to hurt you, and now you're gonna pretend like you don't care. We can't move forward if we're not honest with each other. It's the least we should do for Willa."

Chin high, she left the pavilion to walk under the giant oak trees. Lights draped from the branches and long clusters hung in uneven lines. "I promise not to do anything to embarrass you."

"Not once in our whole life have you embarrassed me. So don't use that to hide behind. Not with me." He followed but gave her space. "Cat, I'm worried."

She turned in a slow circle, her face tipped to the night sky. Even lost and unfocused, she was grace and elegance. "I'm fine." Pulling the lapels of his jacket closer, she buried her nose into the shoulder and took a deep breath.

"Catalina. What happened?"

She walked to a bench that had a faux deer standing behind it. "You think you know me so well." She petted the deer, then sat.

"Because I do. We might not have seen each other for years, but I still know you probably better than I know anyone else."

"You've always thought you know what's best for everyone. You know what, Deputy Sanchez?" She pointed a finger at him. "You don't know me. Not anymore. I'm an independent woman who can stand up for herself. I'm a mother. That changes a person."

"I know it does. And I see the changes in you. You're an amazing woman. Why are you doing this? Someone hurt you, and now you're snapping at me. I thought we were over this. You agreed to talk to me about anything."

She closed her eyes. When she opened them, tears hugged her bottom lids. Her lips were pressed close together.

His girl was so stubborn. She was either gonna trust him or not.

There wasn't anything else left for him to do. He sat next to her and looked at the deer. It was up to her to talk and it didn't look like she was going to. They sat in silence.

"You know Mrs. Johnson, right? Yes. You do. I hear you dated Vanessa."

He tried to keep his face casual, but he was surprised. That was not what he expected. "I'm not sure two dinners count as dating. We went out a few times. I've seen her mother around town." He grinned and leaned in closer. "Pulled her over once for speeding. I don't know her. We don't exactly run in the same kind of circles."

She grinned for the first time. "Did you give her a ticket?"

"You'd better believe it. It was a school zone."

"She's always been considered one of my mom's 'friends.'" She made air quotes. "She and a couple other women were outside by the bathrooms." Catalina played with the edge of his sleeve. "They started talking about you and me."

He sighed. "You know what they say doesn't matter, right?"

"It does if you're running for sheriff. Anyway, they love you, and they're happy about you stepping up. They were very concerned about the drama I would bring into your life. Then they went after Willa."

His jaws clenched. The idea that they thought they had the right to talk about any of them was wrong, but Willa was a little kid.

"There will always be people that get their kicks putting other people down. We can't let them rule our emotions or our lives." He wanted to reassure her, but he wasn't sure he totally believed his own words. "Most people are kind and good."

Some sort of guttural sound let him she wasn't buying a word.

She sighed. "I don't know if that's true. I have to let you know what happened so that if anyone says something to you, you'll know. I tried to stay hidden. I really did. I was going to be good and not cause a scene. But when they mentioned Willa, I stepped in to stop them."

She leaned back and closed her eyes. "I actually threw Scripture at them. I told them fools speak slander." She bent forward and buried her face in her hands. "I'm so embarrassed."

He laughed. "Sounds like the perfect Scripture to me. They needed that reminder. They had no business talking about Willa or you. I'm sure I would have said worse."

"No, you wouldn't. You're like my mom. You have the ability to let whatever others say roll off your back. You smile and make nice."

"You think I'm like your mother?" That sat him back. He never thought he had anything in common with Laura Wimberly. He frowned at the thought. Always being polite was just good manners.

"Scripture. Really? From me?" She made a face. "But I did my best to evoke Laura Wimberly. I gave them the sweetest good ol' girl smile and walked past them. I even wished them a most pleasant evening. I'd like to believe she'd be proud."

"I know I am."

She shook her head. "I should go as far away as possible. I'll only hurt your chances in your run for sheriff."

"Stop. Don't let them dictate our choices."

"It's just our reality. You want to stay in Port Del Mar and be close to your family. I get it. But I can't. I don't know how to fit in here. I'll just hurt you if I stay."

He cupped her face and drew her gaze to him. "Catalina. We can't change the past. I loved you, but I didn't let you know. I let you down. I put all the blame on you, but it was both of us. I'm ready to move forward."

Her eyes searched his face. He knew what he wanted, but how to get her to agree? "I would love for you to stay in

Texas. Here in Port Del Mar would even be better."

"I don't deserve your forgiveness." She shook her head. "What I did was wrong. But I promise this time I'm not running away." She pulled his jacket tighter around her. "I'm running to a better life. No matter what I decide, it will be because it is what is best for us. All of us. I don't want gossip about me to get to Willa. It'll be easier for everyone if I stay away from Port Del Mar."

"The easiest road is not always the best road to take. God didn't promise smooth paths, just that He would be there even when the road is washed out. Can you trust me to be there for you and Willa? I'd like to be your best friend again."

As soon as he said the words, he knew he was lying. He wanted more than friendship. She had always been the one for him.

But tonight, she was scared and about to bolt. For now, friendship was the only thing she would take from him. If that.

He stood and offered his hand. "Are you ready to go back in? We have more friends than adversaries, I promise."

Grabbing his hand, she rolled her eyes. "You do. Not me."

He tucked her hand into his arm. "If they're against you, then they're against me. In this area, we're one. We're Willa's parents. They won't divide us."

He paused at the end of the corridor. "Catalina, it's up to us to decide what our family will look like. We're co-parents and friends, right?"

Holding his breath, he waited for her to agree. He wanted more, but if she was willing to start there, at least he would be close enough to lay the foundation.

On his arm, she reentered the ballroom, her head lifted. He led her straight to the dance floor, where a country waltz was playing.

The evening had been full of highs and lows. To have a second chance at being his friend was a blessing. He spun her and the lights blurred. He had always made her feel safe and beautiful in a world that didn't understand her.

She wanted so much more from him than a friendly co-parenting relationship, but after what she had done, it wasn't fair to expect him to love her again. If he was willing to forgive her and go back to being friends she should be happy with that. She had to. It was only right.

Lifting his arm, he spun her one last time as the song ended. Tucking her hand into the crook of his arm, he escorted her back to the tables of auction items. "This is our last chance to win the items we want. I have my eyes on that basket from the Espinoza sisters' bakery. I don't know what they do, but their pastries and empanadas make my mouth sing. It's not Christmas morning without them. Did you have your heart set on anything?"

"I've never been in a helicopter or seen the ranch from a bird's-eye view."

"You don't have to bid on that. Your father does own the helicopter."

"Yes. But I want to see it with a certain pilot and it's for a good cause."

He grinned and added his name to the bakery basket again, then walked over to her. He signed her name, then handed her the pen. "Put the amount."

He led them through the crowds.

If she lived on the ranch, that would make Andres and Willa happy. Her parents and the Sanchez family wanted Willa and her here. But it would be like moving backward in her life and career.

In Port Del Mar she was forever destined to be the messed-up Wimberly kid. The night her father saw Andres leaving her room, she had had the chance to fight for their future, but she hadn't.

In Austin, she could avoid the small-town gossip and Andres would be able to see Willa more than if she was in Canada.

She loved him so much there was no point in lying to herself. But what would be the best for him? Probably leaving Willa with him and disappearing to Canada would make everyone happy.

But she couldn't do that. There was no way she could leave her daughter behind. Not to have her in her life was unimaginable. She stumbled, shocked at the implications of that thought. That was exactly what she was asking of Andres.

A painful cry escaped before she could stop it.

"Cat, are you okay?"

No. "Sorry. I'm fine. I just need to sit."

He took her to their table, then left to get her water. She watched him disappear into the crowd. He would always be her daughter's father, but nothing more to her.

She'd turn down the promotion and stay in Austin. Or move to San Antonio. That would bring her and Willa closer, but not in Port Del Mar. That would be the best for everyone. With the decision made, rocks sat at the pit of her stomach.

They would be co-parents and when

Andres fell in love and decided to marry someone else, she would be sitting on the sidelines watching with the broken pieces of her heart. But Willa would be there— that would make it worth every hurt.

Chapter Fourteen

The sun refused to be ignored any longer. Cat glanced at her phone with one eye closed. Then she shot straight up from her bed. It was after ten. She never slept this late.

She had expected Willa to come charging in demanding details of the night before.

After last night's excitement and emotional decision-making, it was hard to get out of bed. Soon she would be getting a phone call offering her the job of a lifetime, and she'd turn it down.

Willa and Andres deserved a chance to

develop a real father-daughter relationship. They couldn't do that with fifteen hundred miles between them.

She flopped back on her rumpled blankets, proof of her restless night. Her parents must have kept Willa away. Jumping out of bed, she rushed to get dressed and find her daughter.

After several failed attempts, she went into her father's study. Curled up at his side was the most precious piece of her heart. Sound asleep.

Her father opened his eyes and smiled at her. "She had a very late night, then woke up early to bombard you with questions. I heroically distracted her by looking at old pictures." With total devotion he gazed at Willa. "You know the sad part is that I don't remember ever holding you like this."

"I never sat still long enough."

"That's true. You know, when she was born so active, I was..." He sighed. "I was worried that she would have some of the issues you had. Your mother and I looked up early signs of dyslexia and ADD. I didn't want to make the same mistakes."

Tears welled in her eyes. "Daddy…"

"I've been wanting to tell you, but I… Well, I don't like admitting I'm wrong. I'm sorry I told you it was something you could get over."

"Thank you." She took his hand. It had always been so strong and big, but now it had a slight tremor. "It means a lot to me to hear you say this." More than she had realized.

He made a gruff sound. "Made me think of my grandpa, your great-grandpa Clyde. He was a cowboy's cowboy. When it came to the land and horses, no one was smarter."

He turned and looked out the floor-to-ceiling windows that overlooked the big sky that covered their land. "When I was little, we'd spend hours on the horses or in his old truck, going over the pastures and the fences. Checking on the stock. He loved this ranch." He chuckled.

"What he hated was sitting still and school. He said college was a waste of time. All that fancy learning only messed with the mind."

He brought his gaze back to her and squeezed her hand. "Looking back, I believe Grandpa struggled with reading and sitting still. I didn't think much about it at the time, but he and my grandma had a routine in the morning. While he ate his breakfast and drank his coffee, she'd read the newspaper to him, or they would go over any important papers for the ranch. I thought it was just something they did together. I'm sorry. We did so many things wrong. You were a child. It's completely on me and your mother."

She was going to start sobbing. Never in a million years did she think she'd hear any sort of apology from her father. Not the proud and always-right Calvin Wimberly.

Leaning over his bed, she hugged him

for a long moment. "Daddy, this means more to me than I can ever say."

He nodded, then kissed Willa's head. She was still sound asleep. "When everything happened with you and Andres, I'm sorry I sent you away. That I..."

He looked up at her, his eyes watery. "I have so many regrets." His arm went around Willa, and he pulled the sleeping child closer. "Each day when I do my prayers, I thank God you were strong enough to stand up to me and tell me no. You're a fierce mother. Willa is blessed to have you."

Her father was crying. Never, not once in her life, had she seen him cry.

"It's okay, Daddy." Laying a hand on his shoulder, she tried to comfort him. "You were just trying to fix the problem the only way you knew. That's what you do. You fix things."

"But you just needed our support and help. You're not a problem to be fixed. Andres always knew that. He saw the amazing person your mom and I overlooked. We didn't take the time to see you. He did."

New tears burned her eyes. "He did, but I think the whole 'running off with his daughter and not telling him' thing might have taken the shine off. I lost him, and it's my own fault."

"Sweetheart, time is short. Holding the ones we love is all that matters. If you can forgive me, then he can forgive you. Don't give up."

Being so close, his heartbeat soothed her. "I wish it were that easy."

"Don't let pride and stubbornness get in the way of God working in your life." He kissed her forehead. "You and Andres are meant to be together, and I got in the way. You've loved him since you were a little girl. Trust him with your heart."

"But what if he can't trust me?"

"Then you will have to do what I'm just now learning late in life. Trust God."

"Mommy?" Willa's eyes blinked, then she sat up and smiled. "Mama, you're here."

"I am, my sweet bedbug."

Willa giggled. "Did you and Daddy dance last night?"

"We did. It was a winter wonderland. With sparkly lights and beautiful ladies. I have a picture of your dad and me."

"I heard from a little bird that your mom also won a helicopter ride across the ranch and along the beach with none other than the best pilot in the county. Your dad." Her father tweaked Willa's nose.

"How did you—"

There was a knock on the door. Her father called for them to come in, then fell into a coughing fit. "Daddy, can I get you something?" She stood, wanting to help.

He shook his head no. Andres entered the room. Her mother followed close behind.

Coughing, her father waved them off. "Stop hovering. I'm not dying right now." He pulled himself up and sat straighter in bed. "I believe you three have a date with one of my helicopters."

Andres looked at her, then to her father, a frown on his face. "Uhm, how did you already hear about that?"

Her mother sat on the edge of the bed and giggled. "We knew about it as soon as the bids were closed. I made sure everything was ready. And I packed y'all a lunch. Enjoy." She threw her hands up.

Andres relaxed. "So that explains the message I got to get to the ranch house before noon. I was a little worried." Willa reached for him and he picked her up. "Looks like we are taking to the sky today, ladies."

"Yay. Surely this is the best day ever!" Willa slipped to the ground. Excitement had her twirling.

Laura held out her hand. "Come with me and we'll get the picnic basket."

Feeling lighter than she had in months, maybe six years, she turned to follow her mother and daughter.

Then she heard her father call Andres back to his side. She paused at the door, ready to stop her father from manipulating Andres into something he didn't want.

"Deputy Sanchez. I'm real proud of you." Her father reached for Andres's hand. "You'll take good care of them?"

"Of course, sir." Andres's voice had an emotional edge to it.

"Daddy."

"Go on, sweetheart. He'll be right behind you."

Hesitating for only a second, she nodded. Andres was a grown man. He wouldn't do anything just because of something her father said.

In the foyer, her mother and Willa held a large picnic basket. "Mama, we're taking it to the truck!"

Willa ran out the front door, excited. Cat didn't have to wait long for Andres to join her. "My father didn't—"

"Don't worry. It's all good. Are you ready?"

"Yes. But before we join Willa there is

something I want to tell you. Last night I decided I would stay in Texas. Austin or maybe San Antonio. It's closer. I'm going to turn down the position in Canada. We'll work out a schedule so that Willa gets as much time with you as possible."

He twisted around so that he fully faced her. "What? We haven't even talked about it. That is not the kind of opportunity you just walk away from."

"It's the best option for Willa and you. People will see that you're a single dad who cares for his daughter. When you can't come to us, I'll come to the ranch."

His scowl deepened. "I couldn't care less how people see me. You've already tried sacrificing yourself for my career and family once. I'm not letting you do that again. Don't tell them no yet."

"I keep changing my mind. I've given this so much thought. All the options have been turning in my mind like a tornado. I really think it's what I should do."

"Have you prayed about it?"

"Not as much as I should have. Then there is the whole listening thing. That's so hard."

His grin was soft and it did have the power to make her feel better.

"Okay." He nodded as if he had a plan. "Tomorrow is Christmas Eve. If they haven't called you yet, I don't think you'll hear from them until after the new year. That gives us time to talk and make a plan. Together." He took her hand with his free one.

She nodded. "Okay." His idea of *together* was so different from hers. She wanted them to be a real family. He just wanted a friendly co-parenting relationship.

"Come on." He pulled her along with him. "Let's show our daughter the ranch from the sky. We can point out all the places you caused me trouble."

This was a moment to hold on to. A moment in time when they were a true family. Just the three of them. One day,

Andres would find the woman he loved, and her daughter would have a stepmother. When that happened, she would smile and be gracious. But not today. Today they were together, and no one else existed in their world.

Chapter Fifteen

Willa was strapped into the middle seat behind them. His heart melted at the sight of the big helmet sitting on top of her little body. She completely trusted him. "It's going to get really loud, baby girl, and don't worry about any bumps. It's all normal. If you need anything or have questions you can talk to your mom. I'm going to be focused on getting us off the ground. Okay?"

With a grin, she gave him a thumbs-up. He smiled and turned to Cat. She didn't look as relaxed and trusting. "It's going to be fun. I've done this a thousand times."

"The idea of flying is a bit more romantic before sitting in this helicopter." She nodded and gave him a very stiff smile.

He patted her knee than focused on the controls. As they left the ground, Willa squealed with excitement. "My tummy feels funny."

He took them over the large barns first.

Cat turned to Willa and pointed to the corral. "That's where your father laughed at me."

"Correction—that is where your mother pushed me into bull nettle."

Their daughter giggled. "Y'all are funny. Where did you fall in love?"

They stared at each other for a second, then he turned back to the controls.

Clearing her throat, Cat looked out over the ranch. "See the long horse barn over there?"

He swung them over to the right, so they could get a better look at the horses. Below, the ranch's best quarter horses tossed their heads and pranced in their turnouts.

Continuing her story, she turned around to look at Willa. "Your father took me out to see a new mare your PawPaw had purchased. I wanted to ride her. The equine manager at the time had a son that didn't like me. He had messed with my gear and I fell. I twisted my leg and it hurt. He laughed so hard, in a mean way. When I confronted him, he just called me a bunch of really rude names."

She reached over and touched his arm. "Your father helped me up, then put that boy in his place. Your dad never liked bullies. The kid was older and taller than us both, but your dad was my hero. Not sure what your father told him, but he never bothered me again. I knew that I could always count on your dad."

Willa asked for more stories about them riding together as he flew over the pastures where the cattle grazed. They saw his father working on a water pump at one of the stock tanks. Then they buzzed his house.

"Look, it's Buelita!" She came out of the house and waved at them.

"I fell in love with your mom in Buelita's kitchen."

A soft gasp came from Cat, but he didn't dare look at her.

"Was she cooking for you?"

He laughed. "Trying to, and dancing. She had always loved dancing and I wanted to see her that happy all the time. It made me happy." Just like now. Why was he being so stubborn? He loved her and always would.

Flying low over the beach they moved along with a pod of dolphins. Willa squealed with delight. He had his family with him and they were flying together.

This was the life he dreamed of. He wanted them to stay right here in Port Del Mar with him. But he settled for a simple question. "Ready to eat?"

"No! I want to fly more!" Willa clapped.

"What about playing on the beach?"

"Yes!" She clapped again.

He came to a grassy area not far from where the ranch met the ocean and set the chopper down. Once the rotors stopped, he took off his helmet and looked behind him. "It's a short walk to the edge of a rise where we could see the Gulf. There's a trail down to the beach. Want to go there first?"

"Will there be seashells?"

Cat nodded. "Probably. It looks like the tide has gone out, and no one but us has been on the beach. We have a good chance."

Willa bounced against the harness. "I want to go! I want to go!"

It took a few minutes but they finally made their way over the dunes. Willa ran ahead. It seemed natural to reach for Cat's hand, so he did. She jumped a little, then looked down where their fingers were interlocked. Lifting her gaze to him, her mouth opened and her eyes blinked rapidly.

"Sorry." He pulled away, but her hand

tightened. Stopping in the middle of the path, he searched her face.

"I like you holding my hand. You just surprised me, that's all."

He glanced over her shoulder to make sure Willa was in sight, then turned back to Cat. "Thank you for today. I want more of this. Of us together as a family."

She nodded. "It has been lovely, but it's not the real world." She twisted to see their daughter. "Come on. Let's go play in the sand." Not letting go of his hand, she pulled him along.

They combed the beach, finding several different types of shells and even a sand dollar that was almost whole.

"Mama, look!" Willa had made a large heart with the shells. "Can you help me write our names inside?"

This was the reason he had been restless. His family hadn't been with him. He wasn't living the life God planned for him. He was going to have to trust God and change the script.

With a long stick, Cat carefully spelled out each name, showing Willa how to write them. "Daddy, we're all together!" She added the broken parts of the sand dollar in the middle.

He stood next to Cat in silence as they watched. Was she as moved by this as he was? They did belong together. Willa ran to the edge of the waves.

Unable to hold back any longer, he turned to her, ready to risk it all. "Cat, I love you. I always have. We have to find a way to make this work. I don't want anyone else. We belong together. All three of us."

"Oh, Andres." Her breath caught. "I…" She covered her mouth with her hand.

"Don't say anything right now. The words were begging me to spit them out. I know we have things to work on, but I think we're worth the fight." He gazed at Willa. "I needed you to know how I feel."

She blinked several times. "Thank you. I…" She took a deep breath then looked away. "I never stopped loving you. But that's the easy part. I don't know where we go from here."

Swallowing past the hard lump in his throat, he cupped her face and gently brought her gaze around to meet his. "It's okay. Just don't say no or yes to the job yet. I know words are easy, but if we love each other anything is possible if we are willing to fight this time."

All she could manage was a nod. His words were everything she had dreamed of hearing. But she understood what was really behind them. He wanted to keep his daughter close to him. "I…"

What? What did she say to this? She loved him, too. But was it enough? She wanted to cry.

Cupping her face, his thumb caressed her check. Then he leaned in, his lips gently touching hers. The air froze in her lungs. She'd always been so impulsive. Their next move needed to be thought out.

Putting a hand on his chest, she stepped back. "You've always been with me, in my heart, but so much has happened. You have a great chance at being sheriff." A sound that wanted to be a laugh escaped. "Sheriff. Can you believe that?"

Giving her space, he shook his head. "I'm not sure how I got here."

"Because you're a real hero who takes care of people. I can't imagine a better sheriff. You're right, we can figure out all the rest." She also couldn't imagine moving back to Port Del Mar. "How about we—"

"Mama! Daddy! Look!" Willa ran to them with a large black-and-white conch shell.

Andres lifted her up and swung her around to his back. "That's a zebra conch. And one of the best I've ever seen."

"Zebras are like horses. PawPaw said I could have a zebra if I wanted one. Lots of ranches have them."

"You are not getting a zebra." Cat rolled

her eyes. She was going to have a serious talk with her father.

"Hey. Did you know that your mom and I use to ride horses along this beach?"

"Really? I want to ride a zebra."

Andres laughed. "How about I give you a ride back up to the helicopter and we can have lunch?"

"Giddyup," Willa yelled as Andres ran up the path.

Following them, Catalina couldn't take her gaze off the two most important people in her life. Why had she waited so long to come back?

Her heart pushed at the confines of her chest. There was so much love, but life was so hard. Tears burned her eyes. Why couldn't life ever be easy?

"Mama. GiGi packed your favorite! Chicken fingers and cut grapes."

Andres tossed pillows on a thick blanket as Willa dug through the wicker basket.

"Did you clean your hands?" Catalina pulled out the wipes and passed them around. "And I think you have that wrong. Those are your favorites."

As a family they sat on the cushions and dug through all the finger foods. She didn't want their bubble to pop. Andres had said he loved her.

Tomorrow was the dance recital, then Christmas Eve. It was going by too fast. The real world would come crashing in soon and they would have to go back to reality.

For this moment she would hold his word close and cherish this moment as a family. The family of her dreams.

Chapter Sixteen

It had been a long day, but one of the best. Her little dancers had gotten to ride in the parade with their beautiful dresses. The flatbed had been turned into a tiny fantasyland with flocked trees and strings of shimmering stars that lit the float. Willa and Andres had been on one end and she had sat on the other, all the little ones between them. Every time they stopped, the kids would stand and twirl.

The crowd had loved it and had cheered the children on. She had been worried they would be too tired to perform tonight, but they were energized.

It was Christmas Eve, and after this they would be going to a late-night worship service, then to the Sanchez home for tamales. This was more than she had hoped for when she decided to bring Willa home for Christmas. In a few weeks, she'd be leaving again. She blocked that thought and focused on the dancers in front of her.

They were backstage getting ready to showcase all the hard work they had put into their tiny little version of *The Nutcracker*. Hair was being fixed and shoes secured. She looked at the girls and boys, who were glowing with excitement. She couldn't believe that someone across the bridge had decided they weren't good enough to dance. Amy Patterson came up to Catalina. "They're so excited. I'll stay backstage, ready to help if anything goes wrong or someone needs to make a quick exit."

Amy was a local college student who had danced her whole life. Now she was working on a degree in dance and special education. She'd be taking over their little troupe when Catalina left. Nope. Not going there.

She was going to live in the moment. For her dancers, it was the grandest of opening nights.

Her heart was pounding as if it was a real performance in front of a Houston audience.

Andres came in next to her and took her hand. "This is going to be great."

The small historical opera house was full of parents and other townspeople. "You know, ironically my great-great-grandparents donated the money to build this, along with the original one-room school and church."

He chuckled. "And now both of those buildings are part of the local museum. You do remember I went to elementary here, right? It was part of our yearly field trips. We were told that Mabel Wimberly was determined to bring civilization to the wild Texas coast. She wanted it to rival Galveston."

"Did they tell you that the reason our main house got so big was because Mabel and her husband, August, fought about that and it got so bad they refused to be in the same room together? He did not want a dime of his money being wasted on silly stuff like the arts and education. Mabel was the only child of a wealthy business-man, so she had her own money. It was her family money that made the ranch as large as it is today."

"Wow. That was not part of the tour. So you took after your grandma Mabel, and your dad was in the other camp?"

"In this tour, do they mention that the Wimberly family has a long history of stubbornness?"

He laughed. "Not that I recall, but I might have picked up on that all by my-self." Andres took her hand. "You have every right to be proud of your family leg-acy. But you can still be your own person."

"How do I do that?"

He raised a brow.

"Daddy!" Willa tackled him. "When are we going to dance?" The other children clustered around them, giggling and bouncing with excitement.

Their conversation was over.

She waved her hands to calm them down. "You all worked very hard for this. When I count to five, Miss Amy will put everyone in place. Are you ready? Any last questions?"

Lucy De La Rosa raised her hand. "I need to go to the restroom."

Oh no. She glanced around. What would be worse, starting late or having an accident on the stage? "Hurry, sweetheart."

Quinn, her stepfather, picked up the little girl as he ran to the side door. He looked over his shoulder. "We'll be right back."

Andres and Elijah laughed. "That's a father of five kids."

The three men wore identical toy soldier outfits. Quinn Sinclair and Elijah De La Rosa were brothers-in-law. Quinn had a son and daughter in the troupe, and Elijah's daughter was her oldest and best dancer.

During the rehearsal, the kids had all said they wanted to leap high into the air. The three men had volunteered without question when she asked for help. They framed the stage and dancers like strong columns. Each looked dashing.

She scanned the rest of her twelve little dancers. "Okay. Everyone else is ready?"

They all nodded. She lifted her hands. "Let's do a few stretches. And you remember the most important part?"

"To have fun!" they all said as one.

"Everyone sitting out there is here to support you and cheer you on."

Lucy rushed back to the others. Quinn was right behind her, tying the ribbon around her waist. He wasn't even out of breath. "Mission accomplished."

Cat nodded and stood straight. Her

hands folded in front of her, she smiled at each of her little dancers. "I will take my place." She stepped out to the floor in front of the stage to greet everyone. She scanned the audience. For a moment, her throat closed up.

Sitting in the front row to the left was her dad in a wheelchair, holding flowers. Then her mom and Trevor. Trevor told her he was coming, but her parents were here, too.

They had never been to a single show that she was in, but here they were.

With a nod, she bowed, then straightened. She scanned the room, looking at the faces of the parents, siblings, grandparents and friends of her little dancers. This community had more love and support than she had ever allowed them to show her.

Maybe leaving was making a mistake. Was this where Willa needed to grow up? Could she find her own way in the shadow of the Wimberly name and her past? Austin seemed too far away from Andres.

Smiling, she took a deep breath. This evening was not about her. She would talk to Andres later. Right now, there were twelve beautiful souls who wanted to dance.

"Welcome." She opened her arms. "The Port Del Mar Dance Company has worked very hard to bring you tonight's entertainment. It is a piece inspired by *The Nutcracker*. Very loosely."

There was light laughter.

"We have three special guests whom I would like to thank for helping our dancers reach new heights. Andres Sanchez." He entered from stage left and bowed.

"Elijah De La Rosa." He stopped center stage. "And Quinn Sinclair." He walked to the right of the stage.

Turning her back to the audience, she looked up to the stage. It was high enough that the people could see over her but her students could look at her if they got lost.

A line of children varying in height and coordination levels came on stage. They were all so beautiful. The music filled the space, and she lifted her arms to show the kids to start.

She moved along with the children on stage. Each instrument of the recorded orchestra came together and transported her. The real world slipped away, and for a moment the fantasy swept her into another world, one where she and all the children got the happy ending in all her favorite stories.

The notes swirled, rising and falling, taking the dancers along as they moved and turned. Half went to the left and the other half to the right. Leaving Katy in the middle for a solo moment. There was no thought of her braces as she twirled to sweeping notes that took them all to another place. The other came back together and spun in a cluster around her.

They danced circles around the three stoic toy soldiers. Then, finally, they lined up in the back and one by one they each ran to their appointed dad. The men went down and lifted them high, taking a moment to pose with each child over their heads.

The room was full of flashes, and the men put them down so the next group could run and leap high. Flying.

More flashes filled the room. Four times. Each dancer had their moment in the air. Her heart couldn't contain the joy. It leaked right out of the corners of her eyes. There was nothing to compare to the look on each child's face as they gazed out into the audience from the safety of one of the fathers' capable hands.

There was one more routine, and then the evening came to a close. When she'd first come to Port Del Mar, she had never imagined the joy she'd find here. Not just in reuniting her daughter with Andres and his family, but in finding a new connection with her family.

And dance. The absence of it in her life

had created a sizable hole that she had tried to ignore.

This small community had done this for her without even knowing or asking for anything in return. Dance wasn't about the big performances in the fancy outfits. It was the beauty of movement and expression of love.

Toward the end of the dance, her eyesight blurred, and snowflakes from the last dance rested on her eyelashes. They weren't real, but it didn't matter.

It was snowing. With the last leap from the children, her heart soared.

Everyone lined up to take their final bow. With Amy's help, she had made sure that each child had someone in the audience who would bring them flowers. The children stood in the middle of the stage holding colorful bouquets of roses, carnations and irises.

As people went back to their seats, her father moved forward. He held the largest bouquet of peach roses, blue carnations and purple irises. Tears stood in her eyes as she leaned down to take them. "These are for all the times I wasn't there. I'm so sorry, baby girl."

"It's okay, Daddy. You're here now."

He kissed her cheek, then wheeled backward. She turned to see that all the kids were still on the stage. They waved her up. "Ms. Catalina, Ms. Catalina. Come join us."

Moving to the stairs at the side, she smiled at Willa as her daughter jumped like a kangaroo. She was sure they had a gift of appreciation to give her.

Andres came to her side and gently took her flowers, passing them to Willa, who squealed. She laughed and smiled at him. "She's excited."

He wasn't smiling. Actually, he looked… nervous.

Then he went down on one knee.

Everything in her body froze. What was he doing? "Andres?"

He swallowed and pulled at the tall

collar that looked so dignified on him. He was nervous. "Andres, what are you doing?" There was no way he was doing what she thought he was doing.

His mouth opened and he blinked a couple of times as he looked down, then back up at her. His eyes were now full of determination and love. The love had always been there, even when she didn't deserve it.

"Catalina Wimberly, I just realized that this is probably one of those things we agreed to talk about before we made a decision." He glanced over his left shoulder. Willa was bouncing, her hands clasped tight and pressed against her lips.

"But I was told I needed to do something romantic and was convinced that this would be straight out of a movie." He took a deep breath. "The only thing I know is that you deserve romance. You deserve complete and absolute devotion."

From inside his vest, he took out a ring. The light caught on the diamond. "I want all your dreams to come true. There are some things that have happened that lead me to believe that God has a plan for us, and that that plan includes Canada."

Her brain must have fled her skull. "Canada? I don't understand."

"You have a great career opportunity there, and it seems they also need pilots. We have options and together we can find the future that is right for us. You were right. I didn't want to be sheriff. I want to fly. But more importantly, I want to wake up every morning with you and Willa. I want to read her bedtime stories. I want to watch you dance in our kitchen as we make breakfast and live our lives together."

He lifted the ring. *"Tu eres mi corazón. Tu eres mi amor. Tu eres mi vida."*

She covered her mouth with her hand and whispered the words back in English. "You are my heart. You are my love. You are my life."

"Will you be my bride and share it all with me?"

"Canada? You want to move to Canada with me? I thought… I thought you wanted me to stay here. What's happening?"

"It doesn't matter where we live as long as we're together. You were willing to give up your goals so that I could be close to Willa. But it's not just Willa I love. Do you want to be with me?"

She looked at her parents. They were smiling. All the Sanchezes were there, too. Had everyone known?

Leaning down, she whispered so no one could hear, "You don't want to be sheriff?"

"Nope. You were right all along. I did what people expected me to do. I have a hard time telling people no." He took her hands in his. "You make me realize that I can follow my own dreams. It's okay to say no to people. They still love me. Do you still love me?"

"Yes. I've never stopped."

Willa ran to her and wrapped her arms around her leg. "Did you say yes, Mama?"

Andres lifted one eyebrow. "That's a good question. You said yes, but to what?"

"Yes, Andres Sanchez. Yes, I will marry you. I will be your wife." The last word was hard to say. It was so hard to believe that it was true.

He slipped the ring on her finger, and the whole theater erupted. The children rushed them.

Standing, he wrapped his arms around her and pulled her close. In her ear, low and raspy, he said, "You just about gave me a heart attack. I should have known you wouldn't make it easy."

There were pats on the back and congratulations before everyone finally left. Willa had fallen asleep on his shoulder as he carried her to his truck. "I want us to get married as soon as possible so that you and Willa can move in with me while we plan our move to Canada."

"Canada. You're seriously going to fly

helicopters in Canada?" She still couldn't believe the shift her life had taken in less than an hour. "What did the sheriff say? You told him?"

"Yes. I needed a reference from him. He's disappointed, but that's okay. He understands."

He gently put their daughter into her car seat and buckled her in. Then he turned and kissed Catalina. As he pulled back, he was grinning.

It was the kind of grin a kid gets on Christmas morning when they open the gift they always wanted but didn't think they'd ever have.

"I'm going to be flying helicopters in Canada. It's not all done. There's a lot of paperwork, but they're in desperate need of pilots during the fire season. It's about a four-month season, then I have the rest of the year to do what I want. We can come down to Port Del Mar for long holidays."

He spun her around. "It's like I finally opened myself up to other possibilities, and God laid it all before me. Why did it take me so long to trust Him?"

"The key is trust, isn't it? Trusting each other. Trusting Him. It's been a long road."

"But a road worth taking if you and Willa are the destination." He cupped her face and softly pressed his lips to hers. *"Tu eres mi corazón. Tu eres mi amor. Tu eres mi vida."*

She nodded. "You are my heart. You are my love. You are my life. I'll go wherever you go."

Epilogue

Catalina stepped out of her car. Port Del Mar's boardwalk was decked out with green garland wrapped in red ribbons and lights. A red truck with a wreath tied to the grill honked at her. Bella and Selena De La Rosa waved as they drove by. Catalina smiled before going into Dulce Panaderia

A happy little bell chimed above the door. The aroma of vanilla, cinnamon and sugar, lots of sugar, filled her senses. She'd been craving the Espinoza sisters' pumpkin empanadas since she woke up this morning. As soon as the sun had touched the horizon, she called to place her order. A very special order. She couldn't hold back the grin even as her stomach rolled and rumbled.

"Catalina! Feliz Navidad," Margarita Espinoza said from behind the counter. She pulled out three white boxes. The top one had a pretty blue bow around it. She patted it and winked, then leaned closer to whisper. "The special order is marked. We made them before the rest of the staff came in, so no one knows. We are so excited for y'all."

"Thank you." A heat climbed her neck. Why did this embarrass her? She'd been married for almost a year now. She drove through town, happiness that still felt new after a year, bubbled up inside her.

She took a moment to thank God for all the goodness in her life. She waved to people as they walked along the boardwalk. As she pulled up to their beach house, Andres and Willa were standing on the side of the upper-level deck looking out at the Gulf.

With her job, she negotiated the ability to work from Texas during November, December and January. And Andres only had to be in Canada during the fire season so he was a full-time dad the rest of the year. They loved Canada. Their life was a perfect blend of both places. That might change in five years or so, but for now it was a fit for their family.

For a moment she just sat there and enjoyed the view of her little family. Tears welled up in her eyes and her heart tightened. Yes, her emotions were all over the place lately and for a good reason.

What she knew without a doubt was she had finally trusted God and now her blessings were overflowing. Andres turned and smiled. He rushed down the steps to get the bags from her.

"Everything set?" There was a gleam in his eyes she loved.

"Yep. Mission accomplished."

"Mama, what's the mission?"

"It's a secret, and you have a very important part to play. Come on upstairs and we'll tell you all about it."

Andres opened the door to his in-laws.

"Christmas Eve Gift!" Laura greeted him with an uncharacteristic yell. Then handed him her bags. "You are going to have to get faster if you are ever going to win this family tradition."

Trevor was helping his father and gave him a wink. "Christmas Eve Gift. You're going to have to pick up your game. You are too slow, man."

"Christmas Eve Gift!" Andres finally managed to say before one of the Wimberlys. Calvin laughed as they went into the open living space.

Mr. Wimberly laughed. "I gave you that one, boy." He greeted all of Andres's siblings and parents, who had arrived just minutes before them.

"Now where is my favorite person? Why is she missing?"

"Oh, she has a surprise for you all. She'll be down in just a minute, but first I have a special cookie for each of you."

Together Catalina and Andres passed out the little white boxes. Inside each was a *marranita* cookie made with molasses, but not in the traditional shape of a pig. They each had their own blue pacifier.

His mother was the first to understand. She gasped, then looked between him and Cat. "A baby? A baby boy?"

They nodded and the questions and cheers erupted.

Once everyone settled down a bit, Laura stepped back and looked around. "Where is Willa? Does she know? Is she upset? She told me wanted a baby sister for Christmas."

Cat's grin went wider. "Willa, are you ready?"

Their daughter leaped onto the top of the stairs with her arms over her head.

"Christmas Eve Gift everyone!" Then she bounced down the stairs, stopping on the last one. She stood tall so everyone could read her shirt.

"Big sister times two," she yelled.

More gasps as everyone turned to them. "Twins?" Franny asked.

They nodded. "Twin boys," Cat confirmed.

Noah picked Willa up and swung her over his head. "You are going to have twin brothers?"

Eva laughed. "I thought one little brother was bad enough. We are going to have a lot of girl-time."

Andres slipped his arm around Cat. Happiness he could never imagine pushed at his heart, making it feel too big for his chest. He leaned in close to his wife. "Why did it take us so long to trust God?"

Her quiet laughter warmed his skin. "I was so afraid to hope. Now my life is bigger than any of my dreams. I love you." She kissed the side of his neck.

"*Siempre mi corazón, mi amor, mi vida.* Always. Now all three are bigger and better than I dared to ever hope. Thank you."

* * * * *

If you enjoyed this story,
look for these other books by
Jolene Navarro:

The Texan's Surprise Return
The Texan's Promise
The Texan's Unexpected Holiday
The Texan's Truth

Dear Reader,

Thank you for coming to Port Del Mar for another visit. I have come to love this fictional town and its people. The relationship between Andres and Catalina was a difficult one to maneuver through. Pride verses faith was a theme they both struggled with. I think as humans it is one that many of us battle. I hope I was able to tell their story with grace and love. In the end it is love that carries us through. Just a little inside scoop. *Mi Corazon* (my heart), *mi amor* (my love), *mi vida* (my life) is something my husband says to me all the time. I'm not sure why I have never put it in a book. But Andres in many ways reminds me of him, so he says those to his bride. I love connecting with readers on Facebook at Jolene Navarro Author or at my website, jolenenavarrowriter.com.

Blessings,
Jolene